I0637148

# THE ARRANGEMENT

## COLLECTION A (VOL 1-3)

## H.M. WARD

LAREE BAILEY PRESS

This book is a work of fiction. Names, characters, places, and incidents are either the product of the author's imagination or are used fictitiously, and any resemblance to actual persons, living or dead, events, or locales is entirely coincidental.

Publishing History:

Laree Bailey Press Copyright © 2013 (The Arrangement 1-3)

Laree Bailey Press Reissue Copyright © 2017 (The Arrangement: Collection A)

All rights reserved. Copyright © 2019 by H. M. Ward.

No part of this book may be reproduced, scanned, or distributed in any printed or electronic form.

LAREE BAILEY PRESS

First Edition: Feb 2019

ISBN: 978-1-63035-236-3 (Paperback)

ISBN: 978-1-63035-235-6 (Hardcover)

ISBN: 978-1-63035-234-9 (Ebook)

## ACKNOWLEDGMENTS

There are so many people to thank for encouraging the creation and publication of THE ARRANGEMENT series. I want to be sure to include them all and tell you how this story came to be.

When I first floated the idea on a lazy Sunday afternoon, I was pushing my new baby in a stroller while watching my older kids zoom away on their scooters. As I walked along with my husband, I remember the Texas sun and the wind tugging my curls. Everything from that afternoon, the emotion of it, still bubbles up when I think about it.

You may not know this, but I'm shy. My ideas come from a place somewhere between my heart and my mind, with a bit of my soul thrown in for hope. Because if I write a book that doesn't make someone feel hope, what's the point?

Shyness swallowed me whole when I mentioned to my husband that I had a new book idea. I kept it to myself for nearly ninety days. No mention that it was even brewing in my mind.

I wanted to write a story with strong, damaged women who refused to be crushed by life. I wanted to showcase the vastness of the human spirit, the desire to persevere regardless of what hand one is dealt in life. I wanted to showcase a good woman falling down the slippery slope of morality and how that decline led to the redemption of an evil man. I wanted to give people living in a state of sorrow hope.

All that sounds fun and fine. Interesting even. So how did I present this complex idea?

My husband, Mike, (who programed my phone to say Mike, the most awesome hubby ever, whenever I typed his name), was pushing the stroller now and I confessed, "I want to write a story about a call girl."

Blank stare. Blink. The corners of his mouth tightened and I imagined the urge to not say something stupid flooded him. I wrung my hands and tried to keep my lower lip from trembling while I waited for his response.

One thing about creative people that most folks don't understand is the need to have fellowship with a person who is willing to set them free. Burn all the bindings. Let their imagination soar. Sometimes I'm afraid of myself. That my ideas are too out there. My paintings are too weird. My stories are too strange. Having someone you utterly trust who can cut the ties of conformity (because we all want to fit in on some level), is important for creative people.

My husband and children need a strong anchor to this life. A rock in an unstable world. It's the exact opposite of what I need to be happy and excel.

Mike, the most awesome hubby ever, has always cut the strings. The smart guy also knew from my debut book that there is a fine line when talking about my stories with me. It's an emotional minefield.

I have a file of untold stories, ideas that were fleshed out, but the story was never written for whatever reason. I didn't want this story in that pile.

I could see the path of this tale, but wasn't sure of the subject matter on a social level. Would people hate the heroine? Or would they forgive her transgressions as the book examines what a woman is willing to do to survive? Plus, it was much darker than my previous works.

Mike kindly said he wasn't sure on this one. Making the main character likable would be difficult because it sounded like it would be hard to relate to Avery. My editor at the time, usually encouraged me, but her brow slid up her face and she echoed his concerns.

It was a story I felt deeply, so I wrote the book anyway. When I presented volume one, my husband said it was the best thing I'd written to that point. The characters were vivid and alluring.

The reaction of readers was instant. They loved it. They loved Avery and they needed to know more about Sean.

This led to the birth of my only fan-driven series. Social media allowed me to actually ask fans what should happen next. I presented options and they voted. The story took the paths the fans chose. I originally intended this to be a five book series, but when I asked the fans, they said keep going.

No one can get enough of Sean Ferro. So more books were created. Many more than I ever dreamed.

Therefore, I would like to thank every reader who picked up volume 1 of THE ARRANGEMENT.

Thank you to every person who voted on the path of the books and asked for more.

Thank you to the shy readers who silently supported this series through your purchases.

Thank you to the people who begged your library to stock these books so they were easily accessible to everyone.

Thank you to the amazing narrator, Kitty Bang, who brought these stories to life via audiobook. You sound exactly like the Avery in my mind. It's amazing!

Thank you to my editors and proofreaders. Thank you for taking my books at midnight and getting them back to me before dawn. Thank you for your late nights and dedication to the quick production rate this series required. Without you, I'd be lost.

I've saved the big thanks for last.

Thank you Dad for making me realize that I should be proud of what I can do, even when broaching taboo topics. The confidence I learned to have in my work and in my business came from you. The best parts of my business brain and desire to learn more came from you, from watching your hard work—come hell or high water—no matter what came your way.

If I hadn't seen you power through pain and continue to work, I have no idea what I would have done these past years. Writing became a way to put food on the table when I could not stand.

Thank you for working so hard so I could have so much. Thank you for always bringing home the bacon for me and my brothers. Thank you for the unicorns and girly stuff you brought me when I was sick. Thank you for thinking I could achieve the impossible. Thank you for sharing your stories, the good and the bad. You taught me so much. Saying thank you falls short of the gratitude I'd like to express. I love you.

Thank you to the woman in my life who taught me faith, resilience, and meekness—my mother. Thank you Mom for putting up with me and my incessant story writing when I was a teenager, forever writing and dreaming. Thank you for every Girl Scout trip, every sewing lesson, every Sunday School class, and singing on the pew next to me. Thank you for pigtails and ruffles. Thank you for not believing that I didn't like sparkles when I wore solid black for nearly a decade. It's good to have someone who remembers who I am even if I forget. Thank you for being the mother I needed. You had your hands full with me.

Thank you to my children who know Mom can do anything. Thank you for encouraging me to seek out happiness despite what life threw at me. Thank you for our trips, the jets, the long car rides, the crazy stories, and figuring out life alongside me.

Thank you, Belle, for reading my dark books and helping me see the need for balancing dark and light. You're the person who made that need clear. For that I can't thank you enough. Even in times of darkness there is light, and you reminded me.

Thank you, Michael, for your steadfast silence, your unfailing support, and the look of awe on your face when I say I've not done much with my life. Thank you for reminding me who I am when I get too overwhelmed to remember. You're an inspiration to me and always have been. We're so alike in some ways and so different in others. I'm blessed, lucky, with tons of good juju to have a young man like you as my son.

Thank you to my baby—baby surprise. The child I didn't think I could have. You are the blessing that snuck into my life after I gave up hope...and gifted away the last of the baby items. Thank you for always laying next to me when I wrote my first books. Thank you for your tiny fingers and big eyes filled with hope. Thank you for being supportive in every way possible. Thank you for ideas and your laughter. Your smiles and your strength. Thank you for roaming this world with me and trying new things. Thank you for writing your books. You give me confidence and joy. You came into my life right when my career took off and my health failed. I'm so happy to have you on this adventure with me!

I never wanted to write an acknowledgement because it would make me cry. I'm giving a live presentation to a group of new authors in less than an hour, and my face is streaked with tears.

The gratitude I feel is immense, and there are so many people to thank. People who encouraged me along the way. If I didn't mention you by name, I know who you are and I thank you. I know my first fan. The first person to love my first book and follow me on social media. I know your name. I remember your face and I'm grateful you took a chance on me, and then shared my book with your friend. I remember her name too.

Thank you all, so very much.

# FERRO FAMILY TREE

## FERRO FAMILY TREE

THIS IS the Ferro Family Tree. More of the tree will be revealed in 2019 with new releases!

## MAPS OF NEW YORK

### SEE AREAS WHERE THE STORY TAKES PLACE

PEOPLE around the world love this series and for those who have not had the awesome adventure of traveling to New York and Long Island, I've provided maps of the areas mentioned in the books for reference.

Some places you may have heard of before, such as the L.I.E. also known as The Long Island Expressway, also known as Interstate 495. There's a television episode of two people arguing leaving John F. Kennedy airport over whether to take the "Expressway" or the "Van Wyke."

For people not familiar with the area, things like that can be seen really easily with maps. I've circled areas that the characters frequent throughout the series.

This also makes an excellent resource for a self-guided Ferro tour of New York City and Long Island. Enjoy!

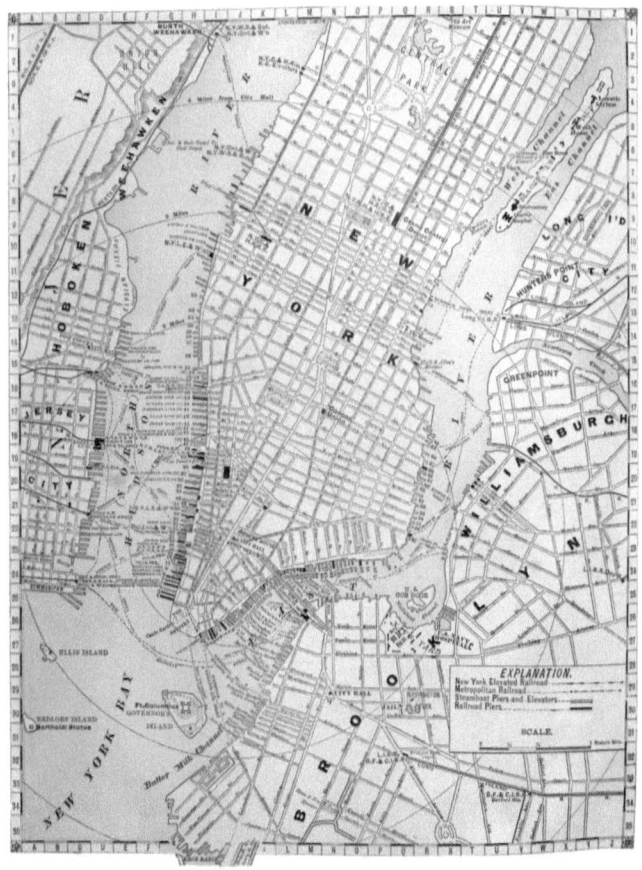

The story moves between the lower bottom right (Long Island) and Manhattan (the land mass in the center). It's helpful to see all the roads and bridges to get an idea of the amount of congestion in this area of New York.

# TERMS & SLANG USED IN THE ARRANGEMENT SERIES

EVER WONDER what the heck an idiom means? Never heard a slang term before?

Below is a list of the most commonly used verbiage in this series and the meaning in plain English.

**Asshat** (v): Demeanor and actions that are unattractively dickish.

**Awesomesauce** (*adj.*): A way to describe something that is beyond awesome with a dash of excitement. Typically said by women.

**Averyism** (*n*): Typically two common turns-of-phrase that were mashed together to create a new, more pungent meaning.

**Babylon** (*n*): A township on Long Island where Avery grew up. There are million dollar homes in on the waterfront to tiny Cape Cod houses.

**Cleavagefest** (*adv*): When a woman's breasts are thrust up and smashed together so tightly that it infers a sexy party may be imminent.

**Cray Cray** (*adj*): Super, over-the-top crazy.

**Deer Park Avenue** (*n*): A heavily congested road that runs through several towns on Long Island.

**Guido** (*n*): An Italian young man.

**Guidette** (*n*): An Italian young woman.

**L.I.E.** (*n*): The Long Island Expressway, or Interstate 495, is a six lane road the runs East/West on Long Island that ends in Manhattan.

**Skankzilla** (adj): A woman who is part godzilla and part skank.

**Slutified** (v): When the amount of skin a piece of clothing covers is severely decreased to reveal more skin.

**Squee** (*v*): A squeal of glee. Try it. You'll like it.

**Tramperella** (adj): A promiscuous woman who has access to Cinderella's royal closet and slutified the garments.

# CHARACTER LIST

## PRIMARY CHARACTERS

### AVERY STANZ
Sean Ferro
Melanie (Mel)
Marty Masterson
Miss Black

. . .

## THE FERRO FAMILY (MATRIARCHY: The name and money follow the women in this family)

Sean Ferro: The eldest son of Constance.

Peter Ferro Granz: The middle child of Constance.

Jonathan Ferro: The youngest son and heir of Constance Ferro's fortune.

Constance Ferro: The Matriarch.

Father Ferro (intentionally has no name)

Luke Ferro (Uncle Luke)

Bryan Ferro

Logan Ferro

Elizabeth (Crazy Aunt Lizzie) Ferro


## REOCCURRING Series Characters

Amber: Avery's college roommate.

Naked Guy (aka Don): Amber's plaything who is always in their dorm room and seldom wearing clothes.

Trystan Scott

Bob (Trystan's Bodyguard)

Dr. Mari Jennings (Childhood friend of Trystan Scott's) Ferro friend by association.

## FERRO ELITE TEAM

HEY FERRO FANS! I'm looking for a few die-hard Ferro fans to be on my ELITE STREET TEAM.

Qualifications: You need to:

1. 🤍 the Ferro family.

2. Have a favorite Ferro who you know everything about.

3. Read all the Ferro books.

4. Consider yourself a Ferro expert.

5. Be willing & ready to take action—that could be anything from posting a review of a new title on Goodreads, to spearheading a Ferro fun night on FB, to leading the Netflix push for our movie, to ushering at a live Ferro event. Basically you can't shut up about the Ferro family and would squee with glee to be involved in official HM Ward activities (online and/ or off).

I just can't do everything by myself. It's a lot. And honestly, you guys are amazing and fun. A small crew of die-hard, I-know-everything-Ferro folks is just what we need!

Those involved get access to Beta reading, ARCs, signed books, events, backstage access, HM Ward swag, and more!

If you're interested, read on. 🙂 If you can't do everything but would be the best blogger we ever had, dude! Come sign up. Tasks will be sorted based on who can do what. In other words, you don't have to be able to be everywhere all the time—even though you want to. Make sense?

Who wants in? Come over to Club Ferro to request an application.

# MORE FERRO FAMILY BOOKS

Trystan Scott

~BROKEN PROMISES~

Jonathan Ferro

~STRIPPED~

Bryan Ferro

~THE PROPOSITION~

Sean Ferro

~THE ARRANGEMENT~

Peter Ferro

~DAMAGED ~

Nick Ferro

~THE WEDDING CONTRACT~

---

Please turn the page for a suggested reading order.

## SUGGESTED FERRO READING ORDER

EACH SERIES CAN BE READ INDIVIDUALLY OR YOU CAN FOLLOW THE PUBLICATION ORDER BELOW.

THE ARRANGEMENT 1
   THE ARRANGEMENT 2
   THE ARRANGEMENT 3
   THE ARRANGEMENT 4
   THE ARRANGEMENT 5
   THE ARRANGEMENT 6
   DAMAGED 1
   DAMAGED 2
   SECRET LIFE OF TRYSTAN SCOTT 1
   SECRET LIFE OF TRYSTAN SCOTT 2
   SECRET LIFE OF TRYSTAN SCOTT 3
   SECRET LIFE OF TRYSTAN SCOTT 4
   SECRET LIFE OF TRYSTAN SCOTT 5
   THE ARRANGEMENT 7
   THE ARRANGEMENT 8

*For Mike, the most awesome hubby ever, my blue-eyed, dark haired hero.*

# THE ARRANGEMENT

COLLECTION A (VOL. 1-3)

# 1

THE GUNSHOTS ECHO in my mind as I stare out a window, perched on the top floor of the large estate house. Down below there's a great pool with a glittering blue bottom. Warm lights illuminate the otherwise inky night, creating a soft cast of golden light from beneath the water. The surface ripples as crimson streamers seep from the two bodies floating face down in the water.

My heart lodges in my throat as a shiver rakes my spine. Time stops as I forget to breathe. It can't be. No. No. No. Unblinking, I stare as denial ravages my mind. The truth is simple. I know them. I know him. Sean Ferro's trim form, the sweep of his shoulders and his thick dark hair. The hardened stiffness of his stance, the remorse and grief he bore is now absent as he floats, listless. I'd recognize him anywhere. He doesn't lift a hand, doesn't pull his face from the water to assure me that he's all right. No movement.

Reality twists in time with my heartbeat, skewing my surroundings until they vanish from my sight. There's nothing at that moment. No mansion, no towering walls lined with bookcases. The scent of expensive rugs and feather filled furniture eludes me. The voices drifting through the room get sucked into the void that holds me firmly at its center. A single word echoes over and over again in my mind like a tiny prayer. *No. No. No. No.*

The man responsible cackles behind me, but it sounds like static in my ears. My body flushes hot before the center of my chest fills with razor sharp ice. The normal expansion of my ribs feels like nails in my lungs.

Thoughts flicker like candles caught in the initial sweep of a current. Bright bursts of memories vividly appear before being engulfed by darkness. Random thoughts rush at me and then nothing. The loudest of which is relentless. The inner-voice, the one that sounds like me, wildly wails inside my mind as my face remains poised, unaffected. My throat tightens around shards of regret and fury even though I manage to keep my face posed in a neutral expression.

All this time, I wanted to be like Sean. I wanted to feel nothing, to have the ability to be a cold, sadistic bastard if required.

Surviving justifies anything.

That was my mantra. It consumed me. I wanted to patch myself up and shut the world out, but as I tried to learn those tricks from Sean things took an unexpected turn—I fell in love with him. The monster everyone hates, everyone but me. It wasn't supposed to happen.

The moment of denial fades and I accept the lifeless bodies swimming in blood, I don't fall to the floor in a hopeless heap, unable to control my tears. No, instead an intense fury races through me, but it's tempered by something that slithers through my mind—a single thought woven from the last cobwebs of my shattered soul. The delicate nature of it instantly turns to steel.

The effect is like slamming a door. Staring at Sean's stiff body does something to me. It's pivotal. I feel it happen. I change. The spider-web-thin cracks that have covered me for so long fracture. The freefall begins. I know I'm about to tumble beneath the surface of my mind, to whatever darkness lies beneath. There will be no coming back, no recovery.

Emotion drains from my body as if hastily dumped on the sidewalk. Fear vaporizes and gets swept away like a cloud of smoke. There's nothing left of me. The voice in my head, the one that tells me to hope and to press on no matter what, is silent. She's not screaming at me to run, to fight, or do anything.

There's a void in her absence, an empty black chasm filled with icy darkness. Is this the nightmare I've had so many times? I dreamed of getting pulled under and drowning. The water was a noose around my neck, unrelenting, unforgiving. There was no way out, but when Sean was there, the dream faded.

Tonight it feels like that dream is a reality. No one can save me. I may still be among the living, but I've already perished. I'm below the surface and breathing water. That's when the strangest thought occurs—I'm not afraid.

Surviving justifies anything, but the game has changed. I've fallen past the edge of the slippery slope, skidded down the sides, and just burst through the bottom. Only monsters live here and I'm about to become one of them.

# 2

6 MONTHS PRIOR, SEAN FERRO

WHEN I GLANCE at the manila folder in my hand and then back up at the girl by the grave, I assume there must be a mistake. There's nothing threatening about this woman. She's barely twenty, and she pulled up to the cemetery in a car that should have been crushed decades ago. She kneels by a gleaming headstone, face hidden by a wall of dark hair. The patch of dirt under her knees is still visible, but not much grows at this time of year.

A shriek of winter wind gusts, viciously tugging at my coat. Swallowing hard, I linger, watching her like a voyeur. I remain obscured by the massive headstone jutting from the frozen ground that lies between us, interrupting her line of sight. She has no idea I'm here. No clue that I've been trailing her for days.

This woman believes she's lost everything, but she has no idea what's about to happen to her. There's no redemption for a person who burns the Ferro family.

## 3

Avery Stanz, 10:47pm, Deer Park Ave.

THE NIGHT AIR IS FRIGID. It doesn't help
that I'm stuck wearing this little black dress in my
crap car. I shiver as I try to keep the engine
running at a red light. My little battered car is
from two decades ago and stalls if I don't rev the
engine while I have my foot on the brake. I'm
driving with two feet, in a car that's supposed to

be an automatic. The heater doesn't work. If I try to turn it on, I'll get my face blasted with white smoke. It's awesome, in an utterly humbling kind of way. At least the car is mine. It gets me where I need to go, most of the time.

The light flips to green and I botch it. I don't gas the car enough and it shudders and stalls. I grumble and grab for the can of ether. The cars behind me blare their horns.

I ignore them. They can go around me. I grab the can on the seat next to me, kick open my door, and walk around to the hood. I shake the can and spray it into the engine intake. The car will start up as soon as I turn the key now, and I can drive away in shame.

The night air is crisp and filled with exhaust. This road is always busy. It doesn't matter what time of day it is. Angry drivers move around me. Everyone is always in a hurry. It's part of the New York frame of mind. I'm treated to a catcall as a car full of guys blows past me. I flip them the bird and hear their laughter echo as they fade from sight.

Tonight couldn't possibly get any worse. I put the cap on the can of ether. Then it happens. My night takes a one-eighty straight into suckage.

As I drop the hood, it slams shut, and I look through the windshield. "Seriously?" I say at the guy who jumps in my seat. He's wearing a once-blue fluffy coat and hasn't shaved for weeks. He turns the key and my crappy car roars to life. He gasses it and takes off, swerving around me. I stand in the lane staring after him. What a moron. Who'd steal that piece of trash?

Still, it's my car and I need it. After the night I had, I don't want to run after him, but I have to. I need that car. I take off at a full run. My lungs start to burn as I suck in frozen air and exhaust. I run down the shoulder, avoiding trash that's laying in the gutter. My attention is singularly focused on my car. I push my body harder and feel my muscles protest, but I don't hold back. He's getting away.

I manage to run a block when a guy on a motorcycle slows next to me. "That guy stole your car." He sounds shocked.

I can't see his face through the black helmet. It has a tinted visor that covers his face. "No shit, Sherlock," I huff and keep running. My purse is in the car, my only pair of work-acceptable heels, my books—awh, fuck—my books. I paid over a grand for those. They're worth more than the car.

I run faster. My dress flares around my thighs as my Chucks help me sprint forward. My body doesn't want to do it. The stitch in my side feels like it's going to bust open.

The guy on the bike is annoying. He rolls next to me and flips up his face shield. I glance at him, wondering what he's doing. Biker guy looks at me like I'm crazy. "Are you trying to catch him?"

"Yes," pointing ahead, huffing. There are three lights on this stretch of road before the ramp to get on the parkway. If he hits a red light, the car will stall and I'll get it back. My lungs are burning and it's not like I have time to explain this. My car has already passed the first light. "If he stops, the car will stall."

"You want me to help?" he glances at the car and then back at me.

I stop and nearly double over. Holy hell, I'm out of shape. I nod and throw my leg over the back of his bike, flashing the cars driving past us. I so don't care. Wrapping my arms around his waist, I hold on tight and say, "Go."

"I was going to call the cops, but this works, too." He sounds amused. I hold onto his trim waist and plaster myself against his back. He's wearing a leather jacket, and I can feel his toned body through the supple material. He pulls into traffic and zips through the lanes. The wind blasts my hair and plasters my eyelashes wide open. We bob and weave, getting closer and closer to my car. My heart is racing so fast that it's going to explode.

I see my car. It's passing the second light. Motorcycle man punches it, and the bike flies under the second intersection just as the light changes. I manage not to shriek. My skirt flies up to my hips, but I don't let go of the biker's waist to push the fabric back down.

We're nearly there when the thief catches the third light. The car in front of him stops, forcing the carjacker to stop as well. As soon as he takes his foot off the gas, my car convulses and white smoke shoots out the tailpipe. The engine ceases. The driver's side door is kicked open and the guy runs.

Motorcycle man pulls up next to my car. I slip off the back of the bike, my heart beating a mile a minute. I can't afford to lose this stuff. I'm barely making it as it is. I look at my car. Everything is still there. I turn back to the guy on the bike as I smooth my skirt back into place.

Tucking my hair behind my ear, I say, "Thanks." I must seem insane.

He flips his face shield up and says, "No problem. Does your car always do that?" A pair of blue eyes meet mine and the floor of my stomach gives way. Damn, he's cute. No, not cute —he's hot.

"Get jacked? No, not always."

He smiles. There's a dusting of stubble on his cheeks. I can barely see it because of the helmet. He raises an eyebrow at me and asks, "This has happened before, hasn't it?"

More times than you'd think. Criminals are really stupid. "Let's just say, this isn't the first time I had to chase after the car. So far no one's made it to the parkway. That damn light takes forever and I keep stalling out in the same spot. You'd think I'd figure it out by now, but..." But I'm mentally challenged and prefer to chase after car thieves. I stop talking and press my lips together. His eyes run over my dress and pause on my sneakers, before returning to my face. Great, he thinks I'm mental.

Turning to the car, I grab another can of ether from the backseat and walk around to the front. I dropped the last can somewhere behind me. I pop the hood and spray. I'm so cold that I've gone numb. As I walk back to my door, I shake my head saying, "Who steals a car that barely runs?"

"Do you need any help?" The guy holds my gaze for a moment and my stomach twists. He seems sincere, which kills me. A strange compulsion to spill my guts tries to overtake me, but I bash it back down.

Pressing my lips together, I shake my head, and swallow the lump in my throat. Today sucked. I'm totally alone. No one helps me, and yet this guy did. "No, I'm okay," I lie as I slip into my car and yank the door shut. "Thanks for the ride." I turn the engine over and smile at him. The window is down. It doesn't go up.

"Anytime." He nods at me, like he wants to say something else. All I can see of his face is his crystal blue eyes and a beautiful mouth. He's sitting on a bike that cost more than my tuition. He's loaded and I've got nothing. A pang of remorse shoots through me, but I need to go. The haves and the have-nots weren't made to mingle. I already learned that lesson once. I don't need to learn it again.

"Thanks," I say before he can ask my name.

"I'll see you around." I smile at him and drive away, holding back tears that are building behind my eyes.

It's weird. There are so many shitty people in the world, and on the worst day of my life, I finally find a nice one and I'm driving away from him.

4

MY DRESS SWISHES around my knees as I walk down the dorm hallway, toward my room. I'm holding my books under one arm and my heels in the other. My purse is over my shoulder. I have my keys in hand and shove one into the lock and twist. The knob turns and I push, walking forward. The door hits something and I walk into it, smacking my head and dropping everything. It's late and I'm tired. I kick the door with my foot, knowing Amber (the worst roommate ever) blocked the door so I can't get inside.

"Open the door!" I scream and kick it again, but she doesn't open up. I pick my books up off the floor and slip them between the crack in the door. I grab my heels and purse and walk to Melony's room. I knock on the door jam and peek in.

"Hey, how'd your night go?" Melony is leaning toward a mirror, putting on earrings that dangle. They sparkle like sunlight against her dark hair. Her skin is the color of caramel and so are her eyes. She looks like a supermodel. She's wearing a dress that wraps around her narrow waist with a plunging neckline.

"Sucked," I say, laying back on her bed and staring at the ceiling. "I got carjacked again. I really thought thieves were smarter than that."

She turns and looks at me. "Are you hurt?"

"Nah, some guy helped me. I got my car back and the idiot who took it didn't steal anything. He ran when the car stalled. What a dumbass." I press my fingers to my temples, trying to stop the headache that's threatening to tear my brains apart.

"What else happened?" She asks, since having car issues is a normal part of my life. "You seem way out of sorts."

I am way out of sorts. I'm quiet for a moment. I want to tell someone, but Mel has money and I have none. I work my ass off and I still can't get ahead. I swallow hard and say it. "I can't do it anymore, Mel. I can't work and do school. If I don't keep my GPA at a 3.5, I lose my scholarship, but if I don't work—" I groan, covering my face with my arm.

"You can't live. Yeah, I get it." She says, putting away her makeup.

"I don't know what to do. I have a huge test on Monday and I haven't even cracked open the book yet. Then, when the car got jacked—damn —all that I could think was that I'm going to fail the test on Monday without my book. I ran down Deer Park Avenue like a lunatic, chasing a stolen textbook."

The bed next to me dips and I realize Mel is sitting there. "You need a new job, honey."

"I know, but it's the same everywhere. Nobody pays enough. I work until I drop dead at night, and I'm still eating Ramen noodles. I can't stand it anymore."

She pats my arm, pulling it away from my face. Her golden eyes meet mine. "Listen, I have to check in at work, take care of some paperwork for tomorrow, and do a few things. My boss is going to be there. You should come and meet her."

I look up at her, "What? And work at a hotel?"

Mel smiles at me funnily, and nods. "Yeah, I mean, why not? It's a good job, it pays great, and the hours are perfect. I work way less than you and make way more."

"That was blunt."

She stands and smoothes her dress, "You need blunt these days, Avery. You're a mess, your car is a death trap, and you're totally alone. A big paycheck will fix some of that."

I don't want to go. My body aches. I'm over tired, and going out again sounds like suckage. At the same time, she's right. Money would fix some of my problems. "Since we're being blunt, how much are we talking about?"

"More than enough for you and all your bills. What you earn in a month, I make every weekend." She stares at me with those tiger eyes and I dart upright on the bed.

"Are you serious?" I think Mel's toying with me, but she nods. "What the hell do you do?"

Mel laughs and shakes her head. "Just come. Talk to my boss. If you're a good fit, she'll give you a job. It's what you want, right?"

I push myself up, muttering, "You suck. Fine, I'll come. But I was planning on spending some quality time with Amber tonight."

Melony scoffs and says, "Yeah, right."

## 5

MELONY DRIVES a sporty black coupe that puts my car to shame. It stops and goes. The windows move up and down. The heater works. OMFG, the heater! I could die. I slump back into the leather when the heated seat warms up. "I could live in this car."

"Holy hell, we need to get you off the poor train. Did you hear what you just said?" She looks over at me briefly, before returning her gaze to the road.

I nod and totally don't care. The leather is warm and I have my head tipped back and my eyes closed. "You try living with Amber for a semester and we'll see what crazy crap comes out of your mouth."

"Did she lock you out again?"

"Yeah," I nod. "She's probably having sex with her creepy boyfriend on my couch." I need more Lysol. I cringe thinking about it. How I ended up with such a rank roommate is beyond me. It's like the university asked me all those questions on the roommate application thingy to see if I could manage using a pencil okay. I thought I proved that I could use a pencil when I took my SATs. Guess not.

Melony's little car darts through traffic. We stop at a light and she looks at me. "That guy gives me the creeps."

"Me too. It's like her guy radar only picks out soon-to-be-felons. Listen, my nerves are so frayed. I can't talk about Amber anymore. My frickin' eye is twitching." And it is. The lower right lid is going nuts, blinking for no reason. I press my finger to it, trying not to smear my makeup.

"Fine by me. So," she changes the subject, "are you seeing anyone?"

I laugh in response, and then realize she's really asking, "Uhm, no. With what time? If I'm not at class, I'm at work. If I'm not at work, I'm at class. I don't even have time to sleep. Am I dating?" I say mockingly and laugh, shaking my head. My dark hair falls over my shoulders.

"Back off, Cujo. I was just asking, trying to get a feel for things."

"What things? Things that'll never happen this side of hell."

"Sounding a little bitter there, Avery."

I smile weakly at her. She's just trying to help. "Sorry, I didn't mean to snap. Today had to be the worst day of my life. Besides the douche that stole the car, I had the worst customer. He screamed at me forever and then went to my boss. I'm a fucking hostess. Like I have anything to do with his meal?" I press my fingers to my head and lean my elbow on the door. My job is to seat people at a steakhouse. That's it. I have nothing to do with anything else, but this guy wouldn't back off. He seemed to think his night was ruined because of me. By the time he got hold of the manager, somehow everything was my fault. My boss made me look like it was my fault and that sums up my night at work. Absentmindedly, I twist a lock of my hair between my fingers. "It was just one of those days and I'm sick of having them."

"My job is a little unorthodox, but I never have to deal with that shit." Mel shifts in her seat.

I glance at her. "Unorthodox? What do you mean?"

"You'll just have to wait and see." We drive on in silence.

About forty minutes later, we are at a building in Manhattan. A streetlight floods the sidewalk in front. It looks like an office building. We go inside and ride the elevator up to the seventeenth floor. When the doors open, we're standing in an open space. The room is decorated in browns and beiges with little splashes of color here or there. It looks like an office.

I glance at Mel. "I thought you worked at a hotel?"

"I do, but this is where I check in." She walks past me and turns a corner. I follow her down a hallway. Mel stops in front of an office door. She smoothes her dress, like she's nervous, and knocks. Looking back at me she says quickly, "Don't say anything. Just listen and answer whatever she asks you."

My brows pull together. What the hell am I doing here? Mel is dressed up and from the looks of it, we are in an empty office space. There's no music, no noise. It's totally silent.

"Enter," a female voice says, and Melony pushes the door open. A woman in her early forties sits behind a glass desk. She doesn't look up. "Right on time. Come in and close the door."

Mel's voice cracks, "I brought someone for you to meet." The woman at the desk lifts her eyes and sees me. She immediately shoots daggers at Mel. Mel holds up her hands, explaining, "I didn't say anything. I told her to come and talk to you. I didn't breech my contract, Miss Black. I need to keep this job, but my friend here is in the same position as I was and I thought you were looking for someone new."

I know Mel told me to stay quiet, but I can't. I don't want her to lose her job because of me. "It's all right. I can wait in the car." I turn to leave.

The woman behind the desk rises. Her gaze

slips over me quickly. She says to Mel, "Family? Boyfriend? Funding?"

"No to all three," Mel answers.

I stop and stare at the two of them.

"Come with me, Miss. We'll have a chat. Melony can wait here." The woman walks swiftly past me. We move to a table in the back corner of the floor. There is a couch behind us and some more nondescript art on the walls. She sits at the table. It's metal with a glass top. I sit across from her and cross my ankles and pull them under my seat. It feels like an interview.

"Miss Black," I say apologetically, "I'm sorry for disrupting your evening. Mel said this was a good job and I need a good job, so I came."

She nods at me. Miss Black crosses her legs at the knee and leans back in her chair. "How old are you? Twenty-two?" I nod. "Family?"

"Deceased." I still feel the knot in my throat when I say it. I wonder if that'll ever go away.

"What are you attending school for?"

"I want to be a marriage and family counselor when I graduate. I have to finish undergrad and grad school first. I have a very generous scholarship that pays for my classes, fees, and books, but I still have to pay for rent and food."

"You need a job with better pay and fewer hours?" she asks, and I nod. "Are you involved with anyone?"

My eyebrows start to creep up my face. "No, but—"

"Any piercings or tattoos?" Miss Black's eyes sweep over me, like she's looking for them through my dress.

"No," I blurt out, confused. What does it matter if a hotel clerk has tattoos?

"And I'm guessing that's the best dress and shoes you own." I nod, not wanting to answer. It's all I could afford. I thought I looked nice, but I was already at work and then there was the thing with my car. "If you work for us, we expect you to have a certain kind of attire. There are stores where you have to shop. It's not optional. Is that a problem?"

"Only if I can't afford to shop there."

She smiles, "Oh, you'll be able to afford it. Listen. You seem like the type of girl we are looking for—no attachments, driven, hardworking, and ethical." I try not to smile. I still don't know what the job is, but my heart starts to race like I want it very badly. Miss Black takes a card from her pocket and slips it across the table to me. "That is starting salary. It's paid weekly, in cash."

A warning bell is chiming softly in my head before I glance at the card. Cash, why is it cash? Some companies hire extra staff off the books. It shouldn't spook me, but it does when I lift the card. My jaw drops open. "This is more money than I make in a month." Holy shit! Mel wasn't exaggerating.

"I know, and that's just to start. It goes up from there. Those who perform well are paid well."

I stare at the card and the massive number. I've got to be missing something. I look up and ask, "What's my job?"

Miss Black grins and places her palms together. She points her index fingers at me. "Ah, that's where things get tricky. You see, we are in one of the oldest professions in the world—the matchmaking business. Beautiful young women come to us and we take care of them and make sure they're safe. We're selective about our clientele and attempt to match preferences to keep things as pleasant as possible. Now, if—"

My mouth is hanging open. I blink as she speaks, thinking that I must be misunderstanding, but the longer she talks, the clearer things become. I find my voice and squeak out, "You want to be my pimp?" Okay, today is totally the worst day of my life. I stare at her wide-eyed. "Does Mel know—"

Mel speaks from behind me. "Of course I know. I work here, Avery. I'm a high-dollar call girl, if you need the bluntness, and from the look on your face, I think you do." I'm ready to bounce out of my chair and run, but Mel puts a hand on my shoulder and sits next to me. "I know what you're feeling, but hear me out. Miss Black is a madam. It's not the same as whoring yourself out. It's more like matchmaking."

"For money," I retort.

"What's so bad about that? I mean, you get to work a few hours a week, get good pay, and have someone looking out for you. The guys have a background check, are guaranteed drug and disease free. That's better than dating the old fashioned way."

"This isn't dating, Mel!" I stand up, but Mel grabs my wrist and pulls me back into my seat. I'm so annoyed with her. I want to leave, but it's because I'm upset. I can't believe she took me here. I can't believe she does this!

Mel sighs and gives me her annoyed look that's just short of an eye roll. She thinks I'm blowing things out of proportion. "There are different levels of service, Avery. You could just be some guy's arm-candy for the night. No sex. It's your call."

I glance at Miss Black. Her expression is neutral. "Is that true?"

Miss Black nods. "We have different clients with different needs. When you begin working for us, you tell us what you're comfortable with and how far you're willing to go. Limits are set ahead of time so there is no confusion. You have a security device with you at all times and check in here every weekend."

"I—" my mouth is hanging open. Getting paid to be someone's date doesn't sound bad. "I don't know."

Mel explains, "The dates don't pay as much, Avery. But it's a good way to see how good they match you up. I mean, if it's the kind of guy you'd take to bed anyway..." Mel winks at me and then shrugs, like it's no big deal.

I break eye contact with Mel and stare at the table. I'm gripping my hands in my lap so tightly that they're turning white.

Miss Black pushes a sheet of paper in front of me and a pen. "This is a list of things that might occur on a date with a client. You can check off the things you are willing to take part in."

I stare at the sheet. There are normal things—hugs, kisses, pecks, French kissing—and then the list gets more specific: stroking, petting, oral sex, vaginal sex, anal sex, and it keeps going, getting weirder and weirder. There are two columns filled with anything and everything. Fisting? What the hell is that?

I shake my head and push the page back to her. "No." I can't do this. I feel like I'm standing on the slippery slope and about to fall down, ass first.

Miss Black eyes me for a moment, like she knows me. "How experienced are you, Avery?"

I freeze, and my shoulders straighten. I turn to her slowly. My answer must be written across my face, because Miss Black smiles at me with that smile people have when they discover something serendipitous.

Miss Black hands me another card. This one is black with white letters. My reflex is to take it. "That also has its own set of rules and prices." I squirm under her gaze. I wonder how she can tell. I hold the card in my hand without looking at it, heart pounding.

Mel isn't following, "What has its own rules?"

"Your friend is a virgin," Miss Black says, pleased.

6

MY FACE FLAMES RED, but I can't move. I flip the little black card over and look at it, expecting the number to be smaller, but it isn't. It's bigger, with a lot of zeros. I don't understand. Glancing up at Miss Black, I ask, "Why is it more?" I thought it'd be less. Who'd want to pay to fuck a virgin? I don't know what I'm doing, like at all.

Miss Black tilts her head to the side. "Supply

and demand. There are very few women your age with everything still intact. Some men like being the first. They want a more drawn out experience, so it costs more. Combine that with a lack of virgins and you are a rare commodity."

Oh boy. I'm a rare commodity. I don't blink. I just stare at her. It's like I've fallen into a parallel universe or something.

Mel blurts out, "Why didn't you tell me?"

Mel looks at me like I've been living a double life for the past few years. It irks me, since she really is living a double life. I had no idea she was doing this. I don't want to talk about it now, either. "It's not the kind of thing that comes up, okay."

Mel stumbles over her words and finally spits out, "How?"

Miss Black speaks for me, "She never found the right guy, is my guess. Avery's been too busy with life, trying to survive. A guy complicates things, adds more danger, and more uncertainty."

I feel numb. That was exactly why. If I got pregnant, robbed, infected, or anything else, then I'd be totally screwed. I stare at the floor. "There's no room for it. If I make a mistake..."

Miss Black nods. "I understand. Don't make a

decision now. Think about it and let me know. My number is on the back of the card. I need to check Melony's stats and you girls can be on your way."

"Have you done it?" I blurt out as I look up at her. I don't know why I asked, but I did. Miss Black turns back to me and nods slowly. "Do you regret it?"

"There are some things I wish I'd done differently, but it was my own fault. The job was great, Avery. My regret is that I held onto the job too long and the result was letting the right guy slip away."

Mel whispers to me, "We can't date when we're working here."

Miss Black shakes her head, and looks at Mel. "Come on. Let's get your stats."

Mel walks to a scale and stops in front of it. She turns once showing her dress off to Miss Black. "It ties at the waist." She pulls the string and slips out of the dress. Mel is wearing a navy bra and panty set with matching garters and thigh highs. She slips out of her shoes and steps on the scale. Miss Black measures her waist, breasts, and hips, and writes the numbers down.

Mel turns to me, "They regulate everything."

"Would I have to do this for the dating service?" They both nod.

"It helps us keep you in shape and pair you up with the right man. We want our clients to be happy. Most of them want a specific kind of woman." Miss Black answers me as she fills in information on Mel's chart.

"Specific numbers?" I ask, shocked.

"Specific ratio. It gives a good indication of curves. The clients will never see your measurements, of course. That's just for us." Miss Black eyes me, while Mel pulls her dress back on. "Why don't you come in with Mel tomorrow. I'll bring the—"

I shake my head. I've made up my mind. The moment of insanity has passed. There's no way I can do this. "No, that's okay. This is too much for me."

Miss Black leans in. "One guy, for one month and you'd be set for the year. It's just one guy, Avery. Think about it."

I don't need to think about it. This isn't for me. "No, but thanks anyway." I say. I flick a glance at Mel and want to strangle her. What was she thinking, bringing me here? And what the hell is she thinking, doing this? I look down and bite my tongue.

Miss Black is talking to Mel about her next date and walks toward a bookshelf on the wall. She lifts a photo album and walks back to the table. Mel sits next to me. I grab my phone and pretend to tweet something. Mel's spine straightens. She knows I'm going to chew her out when we're alone. Damn right, I am.

Miss Black says to Mel, "There are a few new clients who haven't been entered into the database yet. You know how we are with these things. Everything is private, but it takes time. Anyway," she says, putting the thick book on the table, "I'll show you his paper file. This'll be destroyed later."

Mel scoots closer, so she can see. When Miss Black flips open the thick binder something flutters to the floor. It's a picture and some notes that are written too poorly for me to read. I lean over and pick them up. When my fingers touch the picture, I freeze. Those eyes, that face. A chill runs down my spine. It's the guy from earlier tonight, the one on the motorcycle. I pause there, afraid to touch it. A rush of feelings swirl through me and pool in my stomach. I can't swallow.

"Avery, what's wrong?" Mel asks, noticing how I've gone rigid.

"Nothing." I sweep up the papers and the picture and hand them back to Miss Black. When I touch the photograph, I think of how it felt to wrap my arms around his waist. Hell, I already wrapped my thighs around his hips. My face flames red at the thought and the two women chuckle, like they know what I'm thinking. I push the papers across the table toward Miss Black.

The corners of her mouth twitch with amusement. She senses the chink in my armor. "This is a new client. I met him this morning and he was interested in finding someone to take under his wing, someone with little experience, someone with soft dark hair and even darker eyes —someone like you."

I smile too widely and shake my head. Butterflies are ambushing my stomach and trying to fly up my throat. I move too much and practically shake my brains out of my head. "I'm not interested." I try to hide my nerves, but the fact that this guy made me melt before I saw the picture undercuts me. I cross my arms over my chest and lean back in the chair, locking my jaw.

"Very well," Miss Black says, no longer looking at the guy's picture. She turns to Mel and pulls out a few pages. There are a lot of pictures of the guy and his preferences are noted.

I tune out what they say. I don't realize it, but I'm staring at the upside down picture of motorcycle man. He seemed so normal, so nice. What's he doing at a place like this? If he asked me out, I would have said—stop lying to yourself, you would have said no. I wouldn't have given him a chance, and why? Because I don't have time for stuff like this. I won't start something that I can't finish.

My eyes fixate on his face. Startling blue eyes look back. A dusting of stubble lines his jaw, dark like the sexy hair covering his head in thick waves. It sweeps across his forehead, like it's just a little too long. I want to touch it, and push the hair back. Those eyes are too amazing to conceal. My heart is pounding and I'm lost in thought, rethinking the encounter with him earlier tonight, wondering why he'd come here, when Mel pokes me in the shoulder.

"Hello? Earth to Avery?" I snap my gaze from the picture and look at her. "Time to go." Mel stands and grabs her purse.

Miss Black extends her hand to me, "It was a pleasure to meet you."

I nod, and shake. "It's been.." I stare at her, and can't think of anything to describe how it's been.

Miss Black breaks the awkward pause and says, "I did the same thing. So did, Melony, if it makes you feel better. Neither of us thought we'd do it. We both said no at first." Miss Black smiles weakly at me. The handshake stops and before I have a chance to turn away, she says, "We both changed our minds."

I smile at her, completely and total certain. "I won't be changing my mind about this."

I turn away and follow Mel down to her car. I had no clue how wrong I was.

7

MEL STALKS TO HER ROOM. There's a frosty silence between us. It's nearly 2:00 am by the time we get back to the dorm. We pass my door first. I move to unlock it, but when I jab my key in and turn the knob, the door smacks into the couch. Again.

"Damn it, Amber! Open the fucking door!" I'm about to lose my mind. It's the middle of the night. There's no one to report her to, and I am

62

not sleeping in the hallway.

Mel stops a few paces away and turns back when she hears me yell. Her voice is quiet. "Come stay with us. You can beat the crap out of Amber in the morning." She doesn't wait for me to cave and follow her back to her room. I watch Mel's long curvy form walk down the hall and wonder if I know her at all. She's a goddamn prostitute. How did I miss that? Am I that naïve? I suck in a breath of air and let it out in a rush.

Running my hand through my hair, I push it back from my eyes and sulk down the hallway after her. She opens the door in silence. I follow her into the room and close the door quietly, assuming her roommate is already asleep, but the room is empty. We both live in the west tower at the far end of campus. It's the cheapest dorm and the one farthest from everything.

Mel picks up a note next to the lamp after she turns it on. The little room is a photocopy of mine, minus my hideous roommate, Amber the skank. The walls are eggshell white with an industrial tile floor. Mel decorated it more poshly than I did. I could never afford the pretty curtains and thick throw rug that covers the floor. All the throw blankets, lights, and pictures make it feel like a home. My room doesn't feel like that. It feels like the prison cell of a sociopath. Amber covered her half with sparkly crap and my half remains empty, barren, like my life.

Mel reads the note and puts it down. "She's out for the night." There's an awkward pause that makes my mouth fill with cotton. I feel like I should apologize, but I don't want to. She took me to fill out an application to be a hooker.

Mel presses her lips together and looks at me. "I didn't mean to..." she closes her eyes and shakes her head. Pressing a finger to her temple, she says, "I didn't mean to upset you and I sure hope that we can still be friends." She works her jaw after she carefully says each word and stares at me.

"I'm pissed, but I'm not stupid. Why wouldn't we be friends anymore?" I feel a tug in my gut, a warning that I might actually lose her. It makes me step further into the room. I can't lose her. She's my best friend and as close to family as I'll get.

"You've got that look on your face. The one that says condemnation, damnation, and all those other nations where sleeping with a guy is frowned on and followed up with a swift banishment with brimstone." Her hands move as she speaks, flying through the air. She's really worried.

I sigh and rub the heel of my hand against my eyes. "Mel, oh my God, that's not it. You walked me into a job interview to be a hooker. I thought I was applying to be a hotel clerk. They're kind of different, in case you didn't notice. You frickin' blindsided me, that's all." That's all, like that's nothing major. My best friend is a hooker. My shoulders slump forward. I don't want to fight anymore. I'm exhausted and I have to get up early to study, since I have to work tomorrow night. I sit down hard on a fluffy hot pink chair and pull a blanket over my lap.

Mel sits across from me on her bed. She pulls off her shoes and stockings, as she speaks. "You wouldn't have come if I told you what it was, and I don't know if you've noticed this or not—but you're screwed. If you get one C, just one, you're totally fucked. No more scholarship, no more college, poof! It's gone. You're walking the line already in Psych. You can't fail Monday's test. It kills your wiggle room, and you'll have to pull straight A's for the rest of the semester. You know you can't do that working as much as you do.

This is an upper level class, Avery. You're almost done. It would suck to blow the whole thing now."

I stare blankly at the wall as she speaks. I already know all this, but hearing it still stings. I don't look at her. I feel more desperate every day. I can't handle this on my own, but I am on my own. There's no one to help me when I fall flat on my face, which seems like it's going to happen soon. I'm on the downward slope and picking up speed. If things don't change, I'll crash. I can't think about it. I push the thoughts away, unable to deal with the repercussions.

"How'd you end up working there?" I ask, still feeling uneasy, picking at the fringe of the blanket on my lap.

Mel looks at me cautiously. "I was doing what you are doing and falling behind. I'm not losing my scholarship. It's my only way out of that hellhole. When I came here, I said that I wouldn't go back. Come hell or high water, I have kept that promise to myself."

Determination burns in Mel's eyes. My eyes just feel tired. I look at her, not understanding how Mel could do it. At the same time, I hear it in her voice—she can't go back. I have nothing to go back to, but still... I can't do what she does. I want my first time to be with someone I love. I never, even for a second, thought about selling sex.

My mind goes in several different directions. I doubt she follows me when I say, "I admire you, you know. You have more guts in one eyelash than I have in my entire body. I'm going down in flames and I can't stop it."

"Yes, you can," she says, her voice filled with empathy. "Listen, Avery, you don't have to do what I did, but you have got to do something. We both see the crash and burn racing up on you. Change something. Take control of your life so it doesn't happen."

"You think you can control life? What are you, new?" I shake my head and tuck my feet under my butt. "Life is random crap that happens. You can't control it."

"No," Mel says, her voice full of conviction, "Your life is what you make it, and right now you're letting a good life slip away. This is a good chance, Avery. Maybe it's not the way you thought things would be, but working for Miss Black has been a godsend for me. I would have lost my scholarship and had to crawl home. No one said I'd make it. They thought I'd burn out and fail. That gave me more conviction to stay and fight. I'm not living like them. I refuse."

Mel folds her arms over her chest. Her family abused the crap out of her. She was battered, neglected, and selling dime bags before she was 12 years old. Mel left her family as soon as she was old enough, and cut them off without looking back.

Meanwhile, it seems that all I can do is look back. If my parents were alive, this wouldn't even be a consideration. I'd be living at home, eating my mom's meatballs, and having my dad fix my car when it acts up. Instead, my life took an unexpected turn and here I am, fending for myself before I'm ready. I'm so not ready, but it's sink or swim time and I'm drowning.

My voice is small when I speak. "I can't let some guy have me and then take the money off his nightstand. I can't get paid for sex. I just can't. I know you mean well, but—"

"The guy doesn't pay you, Miss Black does. It feels like a date, Avery, a really good date. And if you took the deal they offered you, it'd be better than that. You'd have an insta-boyfriend to walk you through everything, Miss Virgin, which is way better than guessing," Mel smiles sheepishly, like she's thinking of something embarrassing. "I don't know. It just doesn't seem that bad to me. It sounds like dating made easy... and by the way, here's some money."

I smile at her. "You make it sound easy."

"It's easier than dating. You never know if the guy's lying or where his thingy's been. And he's just trying to get into my pants anyway. This is easier." Mel smiles at me.

I laugh. "Thingy? Is that the professional terminology taught to you by the prestigious hooker co-op?"

"Co-op. Cute. Real cute."

Shrugging, I grin, saying, "I try."

"No you don't. You're just naturally wholesome, like butter. In little quantities you're all right, but large doses—"

"You are so gross!" I throw a pillow at her as she finishes the sentence.

We talk about random things after that. I don't want to entertain the idea of working for Miss Black, but it keeps jumping into my mind like a demented bunny rabbit. I start to doze off, and spring! There it is again. And the question that bothers me most is this:

Would it be so bad?

I see those blue eyes and think maybe not, but I can't cross that line. Something inside me holds me back.

8

I'M WAITING at the stop light from hell the next night, trying to keep the car running. It's cold. My breath makes little white clouds in the car as I breathe. I'm wearing an ugly old sweater over my dress, with my sneakers tied onto my feet. I watch the RPM and give it more gas. I feel the car shake and know that it's going to stall out if the light doesn't change soon.

I stare at the light, willing it to change.

"Change already! Change, you rat bastard, change!"

The light remains red. The car shudders and dies. Exasperated, I slam my head on the steering wheel. The stoplight flips to green and the honking starts. I mutter curses as people move their cars out of my lane and go around me. I reach behind me and grab a can of ether from the back seat. Throwing the car door open, I march around to the front. This is the last can and I don't get paid for three days. Damn it.

Lifting the hood, I spray the engine and sigh. FML. I can't stand this. I didn't get to study as much as I needed, work sucked, and now this. It's part of my life. This car symbolizes my life, the damn whole thing. I stare blankly at my car as my insides twist with grief.

I hear his voice before I notice the bike. "So, do you come here often?"

When I slam the hood, I see those sapphire eyes and that boyish smirk. Motorcycle man winks at me. My heart races when I think of his picture, of what he wants, and that he could do it to me if I took that job. He's wearing the helmet, so I can't see his hair, but I'm sure it's him.

"You know it. This is my favorite place." I round the car and intend on driving away. The guy on the bike moves out of traffic and waits for me to start the car. I turn the key and engine makes an awesome noise, but it won't turn over. I try again and again, muttering, "This can't be happening."

I try one last time and know that it won't start. I have a test at 8:00 am. It's going to take hours to get a tow truck, which I can't afford. I lean my head against the steering wheel to gain some composure before freak out tears flood from my eyeballs. My head lightly brushes against the horn. The thing blares like I smacked my face on it. I flinch back, jerking my hands away, but the horn continues to wail. I sit there for a moment and blink before hysterical laugher works its way up my throat.

I kick the door open and get ready to push the car out of the lane. As I throw my weight against the metal between the door and the frame of the car, Motorcycle man appears next to me. I feel him there, pushing with me. The car is instantly lighter and it rolls forward, horn blaring. I cut the wheel and turn it into a parking lot. I'm wondering if I ran his bike over. I don't see it and I sure as hell can't hear anything but the horn.

When we get the car into a parking spot, the guy steps past me, pulls the emergency brake, and disappears under the hood. Suddenly the horn dies, and then the hood drops. "That's better," he says.

I'm rubbing my arms. Nerves creep up my stomach and try to choke me. "Thanks."

"No problem. Glad I was here."

I glance up at him. "Me too. I mean, I'm glad I didn't have to push the car out of traffic by myself."

He's smiling at me. I let my eyes slip over his body and try not to drool. My God, he's beautiful. "Like what you see?"

My face flames red as my eyes widen. "Wow, you're blunt."

"Sometimes it pays off, and other times..." he shrugs.

"Other times what?"

"Other times it gets me smacked." He smiles wickedly at me before lifting his helmet off. That dark hair is all rumpled like he's been rolling around in bed. I try not to let him get to me, but there's something there, some carnal attraction.

"Mmmm. Well, you were out of reach." I smirk at him and wonder what I'm doing. Something's wrong with this guy. He wants a virgin hooker. That's like the biggest oxymoron ever.

He laughs. "What's that look?"

"Yeah, it's the why is this guy here whenever my car breaks down, look."

"Hmmm, and I thought I left my crazy stalker helmet at home. Is this the one with the warning label?" He flips his helmet around and pretends to look at it. The corners of my mouth pull up, but I try not to smile. I don't want to react to him. I want him to walk away and leave me alone. No, that's a lie. I want to know what's wrong with him, why he wants a hooker.

I can't help it, I laugh. "You forgot to take your meds, dude."

"Is it that obvious? And here I thought I was just being a good citizen, stopping and helping the crazy girl with the spray-start car." He's smiling at me and steps closer. My heart tries to jump up my throat and run down the street. I can't swallow. I can't breathe. When did it get so hot out here?

"Stalking isn't usually considered being a

good citizen, in fact, it's kind of frowned upon." I have no idea what I'm saying. I just want to hear his voice and see that smile.

He presses his hand to his heart like I've wounded him. "Is it, now? I thought helping a damsel in distress was chivalry."

I laugh at that. "Chivalry? I think you mean being creepy."

"You know what I think, spray-start car girl?" He steps closer to me and looks down into my eyes. "I think you're enjoying this conversation."

"I have no idea what you're talking about Motorcycle Man. Where is your bike, by the way?" He jabs his thumb in the air back to the intersection where I stalled. The bike is fine. "Thank God. I thought it was stuck under my fender."

"That bike would have eaten your fender."

"Would it now?" A gust of cold air blows my hair away from my face.

Motorcycle man's eyes drink me in before he nods. "Indeed." His voice is rich. It slips over me and I shiver. Our eyes lock and I can't look away. We stare at each other even though we've run out of things to say. The wind whips a curl over my lips. He lifts a hand and tucks the hair behind my ear. After a second he breaks the trance. "We need to call you a tow truck."

"No," I say a little too strongly. He glances at me. I explain, "I'll come get it tomorrow. It just needs to sit. I probably flooded the engine." It's the only thing I can think to say.

Instead of calling me on it, Motorcycle man nods and says, "Then, let me take you home."

I stare at him for a moment, a wisp of a smile skirts across my mouth. "Ah, but then you'll know where I live, and I don't think we should encourage your stalker habits."

"I can be more of a bastard, if you like. I could drive away and leave you here in the cold, but then I wouldn't be around to reap the rewards of my actions. Let's just cut to the chase, Miss..."

"Smith," I lie, not wanting to give him my name.

He gives me a crooked grin, like he knows that's not my name, "Very well, Miss Smith. How about I take you to the general area you'd like to be dropped off. If that's too creepy, I could call you a cab, but you're likely to get someone way creepier than me." He's smiling at me, and it's a perfect smile.

Looking into his eyes, I say, "Tell me your name."

He looks surprised for a second and then says, "Mr. Jones."

The corner of my mouth tugs up slowly. He's lying. We're both demented lunatics because we both seem to like it. "Mr. Jones, will you please drop me off at Frist and Lexington?"

"By the college?"

I nod. "Yup."

"No problem. I was headed that direction anyway."

"You were not," I say and follow him to his bike. Suddenly I notice my dress and sneakers, and my total lack of the correct kind of clothing. The dress is sheer. It'll blow up to my waist again. Plus I have no jacket and the weave on this sweater is so lose you could throw a rock through the holes.

As if he can read my thoughts, Mr. Jones opens a saddle bag and tosses me a jacket. It's some kind of microfiber. I slip it on. It's thin, but it's warm. I swing my leg over the back of the bike and tuck my skirt in as tightly as possible. He feels me moving around after starting the bike. "You ready?"

"Hold on. I'm trying to get my skirt to stay up."

He laughs. "That sounds so wrong."

"Yeah, well, I bet you wish I was flashing you right now instead of all the cars driving by."

He looks over his shoulder at me before flipping his visor shut and says, "I can feel your thighs around me. I'm good."

Before I can say anything, the bike jerks forward and cuts into traffic. I cling to his back and tighten my knees against his sides. Bastard.

9

MR. JONES SLOWS the bike in a semicircle at the front of campus. Half frozen, I slip off the back and jump up and down trying to warm myself. The skin on my face and legs is totally numb. I can't feel anything.

He lifts his helmet off and says, "Sorry I didn't have pants."

"If you had spare pants, I don't think we

could be friends." I shiver and rub my hands over my arms.

He smiles at me, sets the helmet on his seat, and walks over to me. My heart slams into my ribs and I stop jittering like a Chihuahua. The way he does it is smooth, slow. Each step toward me makes my heart pound harder. His eyes lock with mine and make me melt. The playful smile on his lips makes me want to know him more. Before he does it, I know I want his arms around me, so that when they slip around my waist, it feels good. He's so warm and smells like heaven. His scent hits me hard and I can't help but inhale deeper. His fingers brush against my cheek as he slips his hand into my hair.

Pulse pounding violently, I remain transfixed by his eyes. He lures me in, so slowly, and right before our lips touch, he stops. His dark lashes lower and he hesitates. I feel his breath slip across my lips in a warm rush. He breathes, "Sorry," and pulls away.

Every inch of my body wanted that kiss. I don't know what happened. I blink and look away. His hands slip from my body and the cold air makes me shiver. "For what?" I ask, unable to let it go. I don't want to beg for a kiss, but I can't let it slide.

His eyes flick up. He holds my gaze for a moment and a surge of heat passes between us. I want to reach out and pull him into my arms. The way he looks at me, the way his shoulders slump forward, makes him look beaten, like he needs me. The reasonable part of my brains asks, Are you insane? She's so annoying. It's just a kiss and yes, I am. Shut up.

He smiles sadly at me and kicks something on the ground with his boot. "Nothing, it's just that I don't even know your name, and then I try to kiss you after you had the worst day of your life. That's kind of scummy of me."

"The worst day of my life was yesterday, if you're basing your decisions facts." I step toward him, wondering if this is a game and that I'm being played. "And my name is..." Rationality says not to tell him, but I like him. He's more than attractive, there's more there. "Avery."

He looks at me and says, "Sean."

I smile, saying, "Sean Jones, chivalrous motorcycle man with only one pair of pants."

He laughs and I smile in response. I step closer to him and look up into his crystal blue eyes. I take his jacket in my hands and pull him to me. Sean doesn't hesitate this time. When I press my lips to his, he kisses me back. It's so sweet and gentle that I want to die. That kiss makes every part of me feel light, like I'll float away. When his hands find my face, he holds me gently, trailing his finger along my jaw and back into my hair. It's a sweet kiss, a chaste kiss, but it leaves me breathless and wanting more.

Sean steps away from me, reaching for his helmet. "Your kiss is addictive, Avery Smith."

I smile at the use of my fake last name, and at the way he says he likes my lips. "Likewise."

I don't know what I think will happen next, but when Sean turns to leave, my heart falls into my shoes. That's it? He's leaving? I don't get it. The only thing that I can think is that he doesn't want me. Dejected, I step up onto the sidewalk. I turn away from him and start to head toward my dorm.

"Miss Smith," he calls after me and I turn around. A gust of wind catches my hair, making the long dark strands streak like inky streamers against the sky. "It's been a delightful evening." He grins at me before flipping his visor shut. The engine on his bike roars and he's gone.

I don't mean to, but I watch him leave until the taillight is lost in traffic.

What am I doing? I'm infatuated with a guy that wants hookers, rather than women. Women can be hookers too, genius.

I have no idea what I think about anything anymore. My life is changing. I feel the telltale tilt as my world shifts to one side. The question is, what am I going to do about it?

# 10

"TECHNICALLY, YOU PASSED," Mel says to me as we walk toward our next class. She looks sleek, with her dark suit and short skirt. I'd die to have her shoes. They're so cute.

Mentally, I feel like my brain already vacated my body. I sense it happening—I'm switching to survival mode. Funny, I thought I was already in survival mode, but I wasn't. Not fully. The thick air, the unblinking eyes, the way the wind stings as it whips by my face. I remember how this feels, how my entire body seems to shut down just to make it to tomorrow. I'm not breathing. My lips are pressed into a thin line and my jaw locks. I feel Mel's hand on my shoulder, but it doesn't register beyond that. I hear her voice, but all I can think is that I'm screwed. If I lose my scholarship, I have no home—no future.

I ask the question before I think about it, "Do morals matter?"

Mel raises a perfect eyebrow and glances at me. "Are we having a philosophical discussion here, or are you asking something more specific?"

"What's their purpose? I always thought morality was there to guide us, to help us. What happens when it doesn't help? What happens when it's just in the way?" I don't wait to hear the answers. I already know what morals are for. I took that class. I know my heart and my mind. I can't sell my body. It's fundamentally wrong, but there's a tiny thought that brushes through my head when I consider it that seems to think surviving is all that matters. There's part of me that's Machiavellian and doesn't care what the cost is to get what I want, but is that so bad? I just want to live. I want the life that I had before. It wasn't much, but it was mine. Now, it's gone. I swallow hard and take off running. I run away from Mel and away from class. I run away from everyone and everything.

I need to think. I knew this was happening. For the past few weeks, things have gotten harder. My life is slipping away. I can feel it shifting beneath my feet like sand. I'm sick of it. I'm sick of everything. I hear Mel's voice behind me, but she doesn't chase after me. No one does. I'm alone. In a city of millions, on a campus of thousands, in a courtyard of hundreds—I'm alone.

Breathless, I clutch my books to my chest and run to the other side of campus, away from the dorms, away from my books and classes. I stop at the base of the tunnel that runs under the highway. I hate going this way. The cement tunnel stretches under the street to keep kids from becoming road-kill, but it creeps me out. I enter the tunnel and walk down the sidewalk, listening to the sound of car engines running and horns blaring.

I turn the corner at the end of the underpass and am back out on the street. I walk a little further and head into a diner, and grab a booth. A waiter brings me a cup of coffee before I open my books and look at the test. A big fat 69 is written in red ink on the cover, a D. This grade will destroy me. It wasn't that I don't understand what I read; it was that I didn't have time to commit the material to memory.

I stare at the paper, at the numbers and the rounded sweep of the prof's handwriting. I feel like the answers are here. One class stands between me and my future. One class. One grade. One professor.

My fingers twiddle the corner of the page as I stare at it. After all this time, this is what breaks me—a fucking grade. It's not fair. Life's not fair. It's hard, too hard to manage alone. I slip the test out of the way, moving it next to me, and grab onto the coffee cup. I watch people as they walk in and out, wondering if their life is as fucked up as mine. I wonder if things turned out remotely the way they'd planned.

No matter what I choose, I have a home until the summer. Then, I can appeal when they pull my scholarship, but the university usually doesn't grant appeals. The scholarship is too valuable. They'd rather grant the money to someone who doesn't work, someone who has family to help them pay for everything else. I don't have those things.

I stare into space as I sip my coffee. Miss Black's words echo in my head, *It's only one guy. And I've met him. It's a hot guy with quite kissable lips.*

A familiar voice startles me. "Cutting class? Ooooh, you're gonna get in trouble." Marty Masterson, slides into the booth opposite me, still grinning. He's my lab partner this semester and is nosy beyond belief. I quickly slap my hand over my test and try to slip it off the tabletop, but Marty already saw it. He snatches it before I can say anything. His eyes flash with concern as he looks up at me. "Avery, holy crap. Are you all right? What happened?" He holds the paper in his fist and questions me like a parent would.

I snatch it back and shove it next to me in the booth. "Work happened. Life happened. Sometimes shit happens."

"But you don't get any do-overs," he looks concerned. Marty takes off his scarf and puts it next to him. He's wearing a corduroy jacket and looks like he belongs in the 70's with that mop of a haircut. But he's kind to me and always has been. I just can't stand the look on his face, like he pities me, like I'm already dead. "Avery..."

"I'm already aware of my screwedness, so unless you have something else to talk about—" Socially oblivious is a good way to describe Marty. He seems like he's gay, but hasn't said anything about it. I haven't seen him with another guy or a girl. He touches too much, but it never feels sexual. He seems like a large old lady in some ways. Like the exaggerated way he moves his head and his hands when he talks.

"I don't, but you can't seriously think about tossing me back out in the cold without a cup of joe?" He smiles at me and flags the waiter to order a cup.

"I suppose not."

As the waiter comes over and pours black coffee into a bone white mug, Marty looks at me with pity in his eyes. "Stop it." I say.

"Stop what? Stop fretting for you? Because that's not going to happen. What are you going to do? Quit work? That's what you have to do, right?"

"I can't eat if I quit. As it is, this coffee is out

of my price range." I slouch and sink back into the seat.

"I'll buy your coffee, but honey, you can't lose that scholarship. Next to nobody gets it and no one ever keeps it. The GPA requirements are insane. It looks good on paper, but holding those numbers for the entire length of your degree plan is—"

"Insane. I know, but it is what it is." My Dad used to say that. I smile weakly and look at my coffee. It's black. No sugar. No cream. 100% bitter, like my life.

"What are you going to do?"

I shrug. "No idea. I guess I'm not cut out for this." I don't mean it, I feel like taking a pity trip, but Marty doesn't let me.

"No sir. Don't you dare start talking like that. You're nearly done. It makes no sense to give up now. Maybe you can shift your work schedule to give you later hours? You can study in the morning and—"

"And never sleep. Yeah, I tried that. It's not a good long term plan. There's nothing..." my words fall off my tongue. I stare at Marty, wondering what he would do—if he would take a job like the one I was offered if it would save him.

"Marty, how far would you go if you were me? I mean, if there was a way for me to stay here, but it was..." my lips twitch as I search for the right word.

He doesn't even let me finish. "I'd tell you to do whatever it takes. Hell, sell pot to freshmen if you have to, but don't leave. Once you leave, there's no way you're coming back. If you give this up, it means you settled for a life you didn't want." He looks at me oddly; his thick hand strokes his stubbled chin. Marty has that linebacker look with thick blonde hair and buttery brown eyes. Basically, he's a teddy bear with uber-good perception.

I don't look at him. I stare at the table and wish there was something else that I'd not thought of. After a moment of silence, I ask, "So, you'd understand if I did something stupid to stay here?"

He smirks, "As long as you don't get caught."

Maybe I'm asking the wrong person? I look at him for a moment before saying, "So, you'd do anything, as long as you didn't get caught?"

"Maybe." He lifts his cup to his lips, and pauses, "But not livestock."

I laugh. I can't help it. Today sucked. "You're such an ass."

"I can't help it. I've got a naturally assy thing going on." He shrugs and smiles at me. Leaning forward he says, "Cheers, baby," and clinks his cup against mine. "Here's to you finding the perfect opportunity."

## 11

A FEW MORE DAYS PASS AND I know I'm killing time. I twist the card Miss Black gave me, eyeing the phone number like it has teeth. Nerves twist my stomach into knots. Stop thinking, I scold myself and press the digits into my phone.

Miss Black answers on the second ring. "Can I help you?" she asks.

I find my voice. "Apparently, you can. I want

to know what's next, if I accept your offer." I know Miss Black knows who I am, that she expected me to ring her.

"Pictures, blood tests, and setting up a profile page is the next step. All of that is done here. Come in tomorrow night at 7:00 pm and don't be late." The line goes dead.

I look at the phone cradled in my hand. This is my choice. I choose not to sleep in a box. I choose to keep a roof over my head. I choose to be a... Mentally, I pause. I still can't admit it, not even to myself.

I dress quickly and run out of the apartment before Dennis tries to talk to me. He's Amber's boyfriend, a short, stocky looking guy that flirts with anything that breathes. I can't stand him. The only person who irritates me more is Amber. I tug a sweater over my head and pull on my sneakers. I lace them, hopping on one foot, and then practically running for the door. Amber isn't here, but she gave her boyfriend a key. Of course, she didn't ask me. I try not to think about it and make a beeline for the door.

Dennis is standing at the kitchen counter wearing nothing but a smile. Seriously. Pants, man! Put some clothes on. He starts to say something to me. I don't look at him.

"Not now, Dennis! And I swear to God, if you don't start wearing clothes when Amber isn't around, I'm going to put crazy glue on your favorite seat and laugh my ass off when yours is stuck to the sofa."

"Harsh. I'm just—" he says as I slam the door behind me and cut off his sentence. The guy is an idiot. He flirts with everyone and everything, and to top it off, he thinks walking around naked should be a sport. Maybe it should be, but not for him and not in my apartment.

I'm dressed comfortably tonight. I have to hitch a ride to get my car. I'm hoping it's still there and the place didn't tow it during the day.

Mel picks me up downstairs. "Hey, you ready?"

I nod. "Yeah, I couldn't be more ready." I walk around to the passenger side and slip into her car. Mel starts the car and stashes her purse in the back seat.

"Dennis?" she asks as I buckle up and she pulls into traffic. I nod. "Naked?" I nod again. "That fool needs to wear pants."

"I told him that I'd glue his ass to the couch if he doesn't cut it out."

Mel snort laughs and cuts someone off. They blare their horn at her. Mel flips the driver off and bobs and weaves through the cars like a race car driver. "I bet he took that well."

"I didn't stick around to find out."

"Uh huh, and with good reason."

Mel drives me to my car. She looks around like she wants to ask me something, but she doesn't. The parking lot is about half filled. My car blends in, well, as much as it normally does anyway. Thank God it wasn't towed.

I slip out and thank her. "I'll see you later tonight."

"Good deal. There's a party at Mack's. You planning on stopping by?"

I shake my head. The wind picks up and blows my hair. I tuck a strand behind my ear. "Can't. Gotta study."

She nods. "You're not going to work tonight, are you?"

I shake my head. "Nah, actually I'm going to give notice. I've had another job offer and I decided to take it." I feel nervous and excited at the same time. If she wasn't beaming at me, I wouldn't have been able to say it.

Mel makes a high-pitched noise that sounds like a squirrel being hit with a tennis racket. She bounces up and down in her seat. "You told Black yes? Ah! I can't believe it! Make sure to add goodie-two-shoes to your profile. Guys like that kind of wholesome—hey! What are you...?" I slam the door shut and smile at her. I wave my fingers at her through the window and hear some choice words through the glass.

"Yeah, yeah. I'll see you later, foul mouth," I say, grinning.

The window slides down. "Goodie-two-shoes is gonna be your new nickname."

"Funny. And I thought you'd go with something more classic." I smirk at her and she shakes her head. Her hoop earrings sway back and forth as her mouth drops open.

"I'm saving those for later." Mel shoots a knowing look at me. It makes my stomach dip, like I have no idea what I'm in for. "When are they doing your kit?"

"Tomorrow night."

"I'm so coming!"

I fold my arms over my chest and tilt my head

to the side. "Fine, as long as you don't make it weirder, because it's already weird."

"Yeah, I—" Mel's eyes fixate on something behind me. She stops talking and has a strange look on her face.

A familiar voice fills my ears and my body reacts. "Avery?" I turn slowly and see Sean walking up behind me.

Mel's eyebrows lifts so high they're about to slip off her face. "Is that—?"

I give her a look that says SHUT UP. "No."

Sean stops next to Mel's window and stands in front of me. "Long time no see, hot lips."

My face flames red. Mel's mouth opens, making an audible holy crap sound. I turn to her and tap my hand on the door. "Better get going. I'll catch up with you later." Code: Go away right now and if you say anything, I swear to God, I'll break your face.

Of course, Mel says something. "So, hot lips? Meaning you've already sampled the goods?"

"Something like that," Sean says smiling. I take his hand and pull him away from her car.

"Get your ass home, Mel. I'll see you later." I keep my hand in Sean's and pull him back toward my car, as Mel pulls out of the parking lot. I know she didn't want to leave, but I'm relieved she did.

Nervously, I jabber, trying to fill the holes in my head. I feel like I'm hemorrhaging words. They keep coming until Sean stops me. When I reach for my car door, he stops me, and turns me toward him. Reaching for my face, he tilts my chin up and looks into my eyes. I freeze. My heart pounds harder and harder. I think it might explode. A shiver slips down my spine.

Sean says, "There are very few things that captivate me as much as you do." His eyes drift toward my lips before lifting to meet my gaze. Butterflies fill my stomach. An insane compulsion to giggle washes over me, but I manage to subdue it to a smile.

"Insane compliments will get you insane answers." I feel the grin stretching across my face. "Let's keep our feet firmly planted in reality."

"All right. How about this? I have never, ever met someone that draws me in the way you do. It's everything—the way your hair sways when you walk, the curve of your hips at your thigh, the sound of your voice, the way your eyes dart away when I compliment you—like no one has ever told you how beautiful you are—everything about you is enticing. Like a moth to a flame."

"Ah, it's cliché time."

Sean touches my cheek with his hand, slowly slipping his warm fingers across my skin. My stomach twists into knots. I want to lean into him, but I don't. My eyes close as he does it. I can't hide how much I like his touch. His voice pulls my gaze back to his lips. "There are only so many ways to tell a woman she's beautiful. I'm bound to run into a few clichés from time to time."

I smile shyly, like I don't believe he finds me that attractive and turn my face away. It breaks the contact with his hand. I wish I hadn't done it, but I can't feel like this about him. He's going to be something else, someone else. This can't happen. I open the car door and slip into the seat. I dig the key out of my purse and stick it into the ignition and twist. I feel like I'm forgetting something. Sean makes my brains melt and I can't think. The car doesn't start. It doesn't even try to turn over. Ugh, slacker car from hell.

"You forgot the magic spray," he says softly through the cracked window. Sean holds up a can of ether and walks to the front of the car. He lifts the hood and sprays. I hear his voice a second later. "Now try."

I gas it and turn the key. The engine sputters to life. Sean walks back around to my window. I roll it down half way, where it gets stuck. Sean slips me the can. "I thought you might need that."

Smiling at him coyly, I ask, "Are you stalking me, Mr. Jones?"

Sean shakes his head and leans against the roof of the car. When he does it, he moves in closer to me and I catch his scent. It fills my head and I inhale deeper. "Quite the contrary, Miss Smith. I go out of my way to avoid you, however, you keep appearing right in front of my favorite diner at various hours doing all sorts of strange things. It's difficult to ignore you."

"Strange things?" I grin. "Such as?"

"You have a spray start car, for starters. That's not something I see every day. Second, you chased your car after getting it jacked, which was something, especially since you had every intention of getting your car back. When you consider that the car has no monetary value, it makes me wonder why you'd risk your life for it. And after much consideration, I've decided you've filled the tires with gold and that is the reason why you couldn't possibly part with this beast, and it also explains why you go through ether cans like hairspray."

I blink at him. Am I strange? When did that happen? The image of using ether as hairspray enters my mind and I laugh like a hyena. "You pegged me, good citizen. Thank you for watching my golden goose while I was away at school, failing my tests. I shall reward you greatly." I'm joking, not thinking about what I' saying as I say it.

Sean's smile slips. "And what reward will that be?"

"You'll have to wait and see."

Sean straightens and steps away from the car so that I can pull out of the parking spot. I've been revving the car engine every few seconds to keep it running. Exhaust fumes fill the cold air, making white smoke.

He says, "I'll see you around, hot lips."

"Oh, you have no idea." Grinning, I pull my car out of the parking lot and head back to the dorm. I'll quit tomorrow. Right then, I felt so good and everything was going right for a change. I didn't want to mess it up.

## 12

MEL ASKS, "But where did he come from? All of a sudden, I looked up and he was just there. Poof!" Mel makes imaginary sparkles with her hands, like she's a magician. "And correct me if I'm wrong, but he looks a little bit familiar. I would have sworn that I'd seen him somewhere before."

We are sitting in her dorm room. Her

roommate is out and Mel is bouncing up and down with excitement. She walks across the room and flops on her bed. I sit in the comfy chair opposite her and pull my feet under my butt.

"Mel, I don't know where he came from. Sean seems to haunt that corner like a ghost. The first time I met him he rode up next to me on a motorcycle and helped me get my car back. It was the night I was carjacked."

Her grin widens. "He's hot and he's chivalrous? Jackpot!"

I shake my head. "No, not jackpot. He's messed up. Sean looks familiar because his picture is in the book at Miss Black's. He was the one who wanted a virgin." I don't know what I think about that. He seems normal without that piece of information.

Mel starts to say something, but her mouth hangs open. It's like the words evaporated or something. I lift a brow at her, like I told you so. A snarky expression flashes across her face, "Don't go giving me that look. Everyone is fucked up to some extent."

"This one seems more so than others." A

memory slips into my mind. I can see Sean's eyes and feel them on me. It makes me heart race. I hate that I have that reaction to him. And his lips... Shut up! I scold myself. I add, "Besides, most guys don't go looking for hookers."

Mel holds up a finger and corrects me. "Call girls, high priced call girls. There's a difference." Like I should know that.

I snort. "Yeah, meaning the guys have money."

"Well, that's a difference," Mel says like it's a valid point. She locks eyes with me and says, "So, let me get this straight. This really hot guy offers to help you when some asshole steals your car, you accept his help, you guys get your car back, and then what?"

I nod as she speaks, affirming her conclusions. "Then, nothing. We said good-bye. I don't have time to date and Sean didn't seem interested, but then I saw him again. And again. He brought me home last night after I flooded the engine trying to start my car." I have that vacant look in my eye that tells her that I'm remembering more than I'm saying.

"And..." she prompts, prodding me with her eyes.

I shrug, not wanting to tell her about the kiss. "And nothing. He's fucked up. You said so yourself. I can do damaged, but not—"

Mel starts laughing and I have no idea why. She's lying on her back on the bed and actually kicks her feet over her head and holds her stomach as she shakes with laughter. As usual, I have no idea what's so funny. Thinking quickly, I wonder what I missed, but don't see it. I throw a thick pillow across the room and it slaps into her thigh.

Mel rolls upright and wipes a tear from her eye. Still smiling way too big, she says, "Holy shit! That's why you took the job with Miss Black! You like him." She's grinning at me now. Suddenly Mel regains her composure. Seriously, she asks, "Tell me, Avery, what are you planning to do when you meet him as Miss Black's girl? Pretend that you're someone else? Pretend that nothing ever happened? Or are you planning on using the SURPRISE! method of scaring the crap out of the guy? Ya know, cakes aren't part of our MO."

I rub a finger to my temple. I didn't really think about that part. "I thought he'd just gloss over it."

"You're kind of hard to forget. You seriously think he'll act like he doesn't know you? Who's mental now?" Mel folds her arms across her chest and gives me a look.

I make a strangled sound and bury my face in a pillow. Okay, maybe this is a bad plan. When I look up I say, "I am, obviously." I take a deep breath and ask, "What do I do with this? Who signs up for this and has sex with a guy that she already knows?"

"No one. There's a rule. Miss Black is strict with it. There are no extra relationships outside work when you're with her company."

"Why buy the cow when you can get the milk for free?"

Mel blinks at me. "What fucking cow? We're talking about you. White folks are so messed up." She shakes her head and looks up at me, totally serious. "If you work for Black, you have no relationships outside of work. There are no real names, no addresses. Everything is done at hotels. The entire point is anonymity and the guy gets whatever fantasy he wants fulfilled. You kind of messed that up since you already know him."

A jolt of panic shoots through me. I lean

forward in the chair. "I don't really know him," I stammer, "I mean, I don't know his last name, where he lives, I don't know anything about him besides that he's hot and has a motorcycle."

Mel holds up a hand and cuts me off. "What, you think I'm gonna rat you out? Get real, chica. I'm trying to help you. Don't mention any of that to Miss Black and stay away from Sean outside of work. He knows the rules as well as you do. Besides, if he breaks them, I hear Black has a security team that breaks his legs."

"Are you serious?"

She nods. "There's a lot of money in this business, enough to keep us safe and keep the guys from turning into stalkers. No one messes with us." No one speaks for a moment. Mel's amber gaze lifts and meets mine. "Are you really going to do it?"

My voice barely comes out. "I have to. There aren't other options. Rent is astronomical and some temp job will render me homeless faster than I can blink. I did the math. I'm screwed. I might as well accept this as fate and go with it."

"Fate?"

I nod. "Yeah, if it wasn't him—if I never met

Sean—I couldn't have gone through with it. As it is, I feel sick."

She smiles weakly at me. "I know what you mean, but don't worry, it'll pass and I'll help you through it."

## 13

THE PHOTO SHOOT isn't what I thought it would be. There's a photographer—an older guy with a huge black camera—and Miss Black. We start by taking pictures of me clothed. They take a few headshots and then move onto full figure shots. I'm wearing jeans and a clingy sweater. I look young. My hair falls down my back in thick waves. They set my curls before we started the shoot.

I feel silly. That's the best word for it. I have trouble loosening up until Miss Black gets me talking. Then, things go better. I feel more at ease. I laugh. They put me in a few different outfits and the final outfit is a skintight black dress. The back is extremely low and dips past the small of my back. The dress is like a second skin. Every imperfection I have stands out and I feel like a fat hobo.

"This can't possibly look good." I say, pulling at the dress.

Miss Black swats my hands away and says, "You have no idea how stunning you are, do you? The dress fits perfectly, and what you think is fat are feminine curves. Without them you'd be a broom handle, so stop fidgeting and go sit over there." Miss Black points to a corner with a bench in front of a bank of windows. The cityscape is behind me. The photographer moves his gear to the new location. It's the only shot that isn't on a backdrop.

I sit down and smooth the dress. I start to tug down the hem, but Miss Black, says, "Leave it. Turn toward the city, Avery. Look out the window and pull your hair over your shoulder."

I finally understand what they are doing. I

twist toward the glass and flip my hair over my shoulder. It sweeps all to one side. I glance back at them. It's a more natural shot, like they're taking the picture of me when I don't know it. The photographer stands behind me with the camera to his face. I hear the shutter click. I glance at Miss Black for guidance, but she doesn't give any so I turn back to the glass. I lift my hand and touch the cold windowpane with my finger, staring blankly at the city. I don't smile. I feel lost. My life is nothing like I thought it would be. I wish I'd gone with my parents that night. I wish I wasn't left here alone. I watch the red and white lights race by below. Life seems so fleeting, so pointless. I take a breath in and look back over my shoulder. The shutter snaps capturing the haunted look in my eyes.

Miss Black has her fingers on her chin like she's pleased. "Very good, Avery. You're done with this part of the kit. We'll do your blood work and fill out the rest of your papers."

I nod, surprised there aren't more damning photographs taken. As if she could sense my thoughts, Miss Black says, "We don't do nude pictures. The joy of seeing the woman in the flesh for the first time is part of the package. The rest of the pictures are to give an idea of your personality, likes and dislikes."

"But you didn't ask me any of that."

"I know. You'll be the girl we tell you to be, which is very close to your natural inclinations anyway."

I nod. I don't care anymore. I change out of the dress and put my jeans and sweater back on. When we get to the paperwork that I saw the first time I was here, I don't know what to check off. I've never done any of it, so how am I supposed to know what I will do or won't do.

I'm sitting at the same small table at the back of the cubicles. The place is empty again. I wonder if anyone is ever here, besides Miss Black. I look at the paper and blink.

Miss Black sits next to me with a cup of coffee. It's black. She hands it to me. I sit up and take it. Miss Black pulls the papers in front of her. "I have an idea. Why don't we write on here that this sheet will be modified as experience is accumulated?"

"That's fine for future, er—dates, but what about now?" I ask.

"Treat it like a normal relationship and tell him when to stop."

"But if there are no hard boundaries..."

"You lose some of the protection afforded by the rules. I know what you're thinking, but it's impossible to know what another woman will like or what she won't tolerate. There are some things here that I thought I would never do, and that I've grown to enjoy." I must give her a weird look because she leans forward and touches my hand, saying, "Don't misunderstand. I want you to feel comfortable, so let's put a progression on here that way he can't skip to the kinky stuff without doing the normal stuff first. Is that all right?" I nod. This is so weird. Miss Black smiles and writes it on the paper. "Good. I think this lines up with Mr. Ferro's preferences anyway."

"Who?" I ask, wiggling to the front of my seat.

"Mr. Ferro, the man who I wanted to pair you with." Miss Black stands and retrieves the large book from the other night. She flips it open and it's everything I can do to not react. It's Sean. Pictures of Sean, his preference sheet, his description of what he finds attractive, and more. "Don't be afraid, Avery. It's only a binder. Take it and look."

I do as she says, and pull the binder in front

of me. Mr. Ferro. Sean Ferro. There is no first name on the sheets. Miss Black explains how they only use formal names. I am to call him Mr. Ferro. I wonder if that name is real or not. I wonder why he came in here, why a handsome man like Sean would want this. I touch a picture, looking at his eyes. My gaze drifts to his lips and I feel a zing float through my stomach. I blink hard to crush the memory and turn the page looking for answers, but there are none. It showcases a man that seems beautiful and normal.

Sean wrote that he prefers a woman with little experience so that he can take the time to teach her. What's that about? Altruism at its finest. He wants other guys to have better sex, so he teaches the new girl the ropes. That makes no sense. None of this does. There's a disconnect between this file and the guy I know.

A voice at the back of my mind says maybe you don't know him at all.

# 14

MY HEART IS BANGING into my ribs so hard that I think they might crack. I step out of the shower and towel off. Amber is screeching like a skewered cat as her headboard bangs into the wall. I so don't want to hear this, but I had to be home to get ready to go out.

I locked myself in our bathroom and put on my makeup after showering. I tie a bathrobe around me when I finish. Mel has a dress that she's lending me for tonight, since I didn't have anything suitable.

I think about seeing Sean, about what I'll say. Part of me thinks that I shouldn't say anything, that I should let him explain the whole thing. After all, we are both way more sketchy than we seemed.

Amber's voice busts my eardrum and then she finally shuts up. I try to sneak out of the bathroom now, before the two of them have a chance to start again. I toss my makeup back into my bag and run for the door. The way the room is situated has both our beds in the same area with a little Jack and Jill bathroom off of one end that we share with the girls next door.

I race by the beds and fail to notice the guy— not Dennis—standing in our kitchen. He has my throw blanket tied around his naked hips.

The guy looks up at me and then glances at Amber. "Hey, babe. Is this going to be a threesome? I'm down with that." He grins at me. The guy is a clone of Dennis. What the hell? I glance back at Amber, shooting her daggers, but she's lying in bed and doesn't bother to look at me.

"Don't touch my things!" I snap at him.

He grins at me like an idiot. Without thinking, I reach forward, snatch the blanket, and run out the door leaving the guy standing there with nothing on.

I run down the hall, holding the blanket between my fingers. When I step into the room, Mel seems annoyed, but her mood quickly changes to disgust when she sees the way I'm holding the blanket. She opens a drawer and pulls something out.

"Oh gross, not again." She holds up a trash bag for me and I drop the blanket inside. It'll need to be cleaned again and I don't want his junk all mashed up in my other wash.

"I don't even want to talk about it. I swear to God, she's the worst roommate ever. The only thing she's got going for her is that she doesn't steal."

Mel doesn't look convinced. "No offense hun, but you ain't got nothing worth stealing."

"Story of my life. So help me shake of the heebie-jeebies and get ready."

Mel snorts a laugh. Her hand quickly covers her mouth as she continues to laugh. "Where did you learn those words? You'd think you were raised in a nunnery. Damn, girl." Mel shakes her head and walks over to her closet. A dark violet cocktail dress is hanging at the front. She pulls it out and hands it to me. "What do you think? With your dark hair and eyes, I thought that color would work well for you. Plus it's easy to wear."

I hold the soft fabric in my hands. My heart starts pumping harder. I'm going to do this. The dress is the final step on the tightrope of insanity. I'm kind of hoping I fall off and break my neck. I don't know if I can go through with it. I nod, not saying anything I'm thinking. "It's beautiful."

The dress has a bright purple silk lining that is covered by black chiffon. The neckline scoops low and the back dips even lower. It's held up by a silver clip on one shoulder. It's like a Greek Goddess dress. I blink at it for a moment. I can't believe this is happening.

As if Mel can sense my thoughts, she says, "And how about the rest? Did Mandy hook you up with a nice lacy garter set?"

The undergarments are inspected by Miss Black before I leave in a limo for my appointment with Sean. Nothing I had would have been acceptable, so I took what little money I had left and bought some stockings, thigh highs, panties and a bra. Everything was on clearance, but the whole thing is from a store on Miss Black's approved list.

I nod, and slip off the housecoat so she can see. It feels a little funny, but I have to put on the dress anyway. I pull it off the hanger as Mel looks me over. "There wasn't much in my price range."

"Well, I'm just glad they had something. That should pacify Miss Black. She just wants to make sure we don't skimp on anything."

"I can't believe how much this stuff costs. The stockings cost more than my entire outfit."

Mel shakes her head and smiles at me. "But have you felt them?"

"Yeah, they're buttery soft, but at that price I'll cry if I snag them." I'm trying to wriggle into the dress without messing up my makeup. It slips over me and I reach for the side to zip it, but Mel's already there. She pulls up the zipper for me and I look in the mirror. The dress fits perfectly. The bodice is formfitting and the skirt is on the shorter side and flares slightly at the hem. If I didn't feel like I was going to puke, I'd twirl.

"You look perfect."

"Thanks," I say, pulse pounding harder. I take a deep breath and try to calm down.

"Have you thought about what you're going to say to him?" Mel steps back and grabs a comb. She quickly pulls my long locks into a beautiful style. I don't even know what to call it. It's half up and half down. Loose strands hang by my shoulders as random curls are pinned and twisted onto the back of my head.

"No, not really. And Mel, if he says no, I'm walking away from this. If I can't do it with him, I just can't do it."

Mel stills her hands and presses her lips together. "You give up too easy."

"Maybe, but I have to be able to live with myself. My body and emotions aren't detached. I don't know how to do this without falling for the guy."

Mel folds her arms over her chest. She still has to get ready to go out later. "Listen, it'll come to you. One of the things I don't do is lingering kisses, you know the kind. They get all hot and heavy. It makes it feel like something it's not. That preference sheet isn't just what you like, it's what you can tolerate."

"What if I cry the whole time? What if I can't tolerate any of it?"

"You're stronger than that, Avery. Me and

you, we're on our own. We're strong because we have to be. We don't need anyone or anything. We got our sights set on something and we get it, no matter the cost."

My stomach curls. She's just like me, maybe a little more battered by life, but we're the same. "The end justifies the means."

"Surviving justifies anything."

# 15

I DRIVE my crap car to Miss Black's. She invites me into the back and pulls out the measuring tape. I strip to my lacy undergarments and she takes it in, approves, and then measures me and writes it down. I slip the dress back on, careful not to mess up my hair and zip the dress up.

"There's one thing that you have to do to keep this job and that is to portray the confidence that our girls have. Since it's your first time, I know how you must be feeling, but all the same, you can't let it affect your performance. Because, that's what this is—a performance. The client wants an innocent young girl and you will fulfill that role. He doesn't want to hear your life story or why you entered this line of business. You are forbidden to discuss weighty matters or your personal life. Do you understand?"

I nod. It's not like I'm planning on spilling my guts to him and I can pull off inexperienced young girl, since I am one. "How am I supposed to be innocent and confident? I didn't think those things went together."

"Well, here they do. A tease is confident and younger women that flaunt their bodies usually have no idea what they're in for. You're to be that woman, confident and craving sex. Use your body the way you normally would to pick up a guy, but be more overt with it. Mr. Ferro will tailor the experience to be what he wants. When you get to that point, just follow his lead."

I nod again. It sounds easy, but I still feel my nerves swirling in my stomach. Miss Black asks me to follow her into her office. She rounds her desk and pulls out a gold bracelet from her top drawer. It has a little black stone in the center of the chain. She hands it to me. "Wear this at all times. It lets us know you are where you are supposed to be. If something goes horribly wrong, smash the stone. A security signal will be sent and help will arrive, but do not crush it unless it's life or death."

I take it and put it on my wrist. It's a little too big. "Has anyone ever had to use it?"

She shakes her head. "No, the threat is clear enough. Our clients know you have it and what will happen if one of our girls is harmed in any way. It's not pretty. The threat alone makes them behave."

I nod and stare at the black bead, wondering how it works. There must be something inside the stone, GPS and a transmitter of some sort.

After a few more words of instruction, I head downstairs where a car is waiting for me. My heart pounds against my ribs as I slip into the back seat of the limo. We pull into traffic. I feel like I can't breathe.

Calm down. It's only Sean. You can do this. My little pep talks falls flat. I'm afraid. I can't shake the feeling, so I try to ignore it. I look out the window for a while, but that makes me nervous too. I know where we are, I know where we are going. We'll be there any minute.

I decide to check my makeup. As I reach into my purse, the golden bracelet slips off my wrist. It's too loose. I look at it and know that I need to keep it on. Glancing at my ankle, I bend over and fasten it around my leg. It fits better there. When I sit up, the car slows and I see the hotel. It's one of the swank privately owned hotels in the affluent section of the city.

The car pulls in front and stops. My chest feels like it's going to explode. I don't breathe, I don't blink. The driver opens my door. I lift my foot and step out onto the pavement. Eyes fall on me, taking in my regal appearance. I wonder if they know why I'm here, and immediately dispel that thought. If they knew why I was here, there would be cops and there are none.

I step from the car and walk confidently toward the door. The doorman pulls it open for me, and I step inside. Miss Black told me to be confident, to move like I belong here, but my jaw drops slightly when I step inside. Opulence drips from every surface in this building. I try to ignore it, but I can't. My eyes drift from the gold gilding, to the large chandelier with sparkling crystals hanging in the center of the room.

I continue to walk. I'm to head to the restaurant on the second floor. I remember everything and when I reach the podium where the maître d' stands, my voice is steady. I am meeting someone. I tell him the name, and am led through the restaurant. The lights are low. The walls are decorated with rich fabrics and candelabras that match the large crystal fixture downstairs.

As I follow the man, I'm acutely aware of everything. Several sets of eyes lift and take in my figure before returning to their companions as I pass. I feel my heel strike the floor and the jolt through my body somehow makes me more confident. The tremble in my hands lessens and I hold my shoulders back. A soft smile lines my lips.

I think I'll be able to do this. I think I'll be able to pull it off. I feel perfect. I feel confident.

But then I see Sean. He's sitting in a darkened corner with his dark hair covering those blue eyes. He doesn't look up as I approach. His hand clutches a drink like it's a lifeline. The vibrant young man I met is gone. I can only see the shattered remnants.

The waiter stops in front of the table. I step out from behind him and move toward Sean. I lift my hand and press my finger to the monogram in the center of his plate. This is confirmation of who I am, so that there are no mistakes. Miss Black said it's our personal signal.

Sean doesn't look at me. The waiter pulls out my seat. I turn and slip silently into it and am handed a menu. I watch Sean the entire time. He won't look at me. Every piece of me wants to comfort him. Something is horribly wrong. I can tell.

We sit in silence until I think he'll never look up. Then, his dark head tilts back and those sapphire eyes lift and meet my gaze. Confusion flashes across his face at first, but it's quickly quashed by anger.

"What is this?" Sean growls at me, his voice low enough to not attract attention.

Fear wraps its icy fingers around my heart and squeezes. I no longer know what I want. I thought Sean would be happy to see me, but he isn't. I don't want to leave him looking so betrayed, but I don't think I want to stay either.

"Hi," I manage, which is severely lacking.

"I repeat, what is this? Some kind of joke?" Anger surges in his voice.

"No," I say softly. "A coincidence."

Sean watches me, trying to sense the lie that he thinks I'm telling, but I'm not. "I'm sure," he says sarcastically. Shaking his head, Sean looks at me with venom in his eyes, "I thought Black wanted my business, but this is unacceptable. Go back to your boss and tell her the deal is off. I'll find what I need elsewhere. I don't condone her actions or being followed. I won't be manipulated." Sean stands abruptly. I know he's angry. He's going to leave. He's going to chew out Miss Black.

"Wait," I say, standing with him. I reach for his hand and hold onto his wrist. My voice sounds strained and quivers as I speak. "Please, don't tell her. She doesn't know. Sean, I know what it looks like, but please believe me."

His cold gaze cuts to my hold on his arm. I release him and take a small breath. "Why should I?"

"Because you're a good man and I need you to."

He stares at me for a moment and then sits

back down in his chair. I return to my seat. He works his jaw as he considers me. "Explain, and don't lie to me."

I feel like I'm on trial. I want him to stay. I need him to stay. He's my last lifeline. Without him, without this job, I'm lost. My eyes dart away from his. "I'm not supposed to talk about me, but since I've already done something I wasn't supposed to—"

"Just tell me." Sean folds his arms over his chest. The waiter tries to come over to take our order, but the look on Sean's face scares him away.

I wring my hands in my lap under the table. Nervously, I say, "I need this job. When I saw your profile, I wanted..." I stumble trying to explain myself. "I thought it'd be nice that we'd already met. I haven't done this before, obviously, and—"

"I have trouble believing that," he snaps.

"Believe whatever you want, but facts are facts and you would have figured it out if I didn't screw everything up. Miss..." I bite my tongue to keep from saying Miss Black's name, "she doesn't know that I met you before, that I kissed you before." I stare into his eyes remembering that kiss, remembering the softness and desire. "She doesn't know, but I wanted to know you more, and I needed this. This encounter may not matter much to you, but it means everything to me." Before I realize it, my hands are on top of the table. I'm clutching them so tightly that my knuckles turn white.

Sean's gaze lowers to my hands and lifts to my face, "Why?"

I can't answer. My mouth fills with sand and I can barely swallow. All's I can manage is, "Please." I'm begging him. It dawns on me that this is what happened and I can't look at him. I release the death grip on my hands when he doesn't answer. Sean seems apathetic, leaning back in his chair as if he's dismissing me.

I take my purse in my hand, and heart pounding say, "I'm sorry. I won't trouble you again."

I stand and walk away from the table. Sean doesn't call my name. He doesn't stand and follow me out. He doesn't give me a second chance.

The limo isn't here yet. I'm on my own. My heart shatters as I realize what this means. Miss Black won't give me another chance, and I don't want one. I try to keep the tears from spilling as I take the walk of shame across the room. Stopping in front of the elevator, I press the button. I wait and take a shaky breath. When the doors open, an older couple slips out. They avert their eyes as is the custom when a stranger encounters a crying woman. I look at the floor as I step inside.

I lift my hand and press ONE. The doors start to slip shut. But just before they close, the door bangs against something dark that juts between them, a suited arm. The doors reopen and Sean is standing there. His blue eyes are filled with questions. He steps into the elevator with me. The doors slip shut. When we start to move, he pulls the STOP and the elevator darkens.

## 16

HIS VOICE IS in my ear. It sends a shiver down my spine. I feel exposed even though we stand in darkness. Sean speaks rapidly, "This isn't the way it's supposed to be. The rules were broken. I don't know what to do. I mean, I know you." I feel the heat from his body and know he's a breath away from me.

I'm not confident, but bold words spill from my lips. "Which makes it better, doesn't it?"

"No," he replies softly. "The anonymity mattered to me."

"I can't change that."

"But you changed the ground rules." I feel him lean against the wall next to me, like it pains him to admit it. "Now what? I don't want to send you back."

My palm finds his cheek. I turn his face toward me and feel his breath on my face. Softly, I say, "Then don't."

Sean takes a deep breath and suddenly the lights come back on. The elevator is moving again. When we reach the ground floor, I don't look at him. Sean says nothing. He takes my hand as we leave the elevator.

A person dressed in a hotel uniform approaches us. Sean swiftly walks past him without a word. I'm being led through the foyer and hotel staff and patrons are everywhere. Sean pushes through the front doors before the doorman can open them.

"Mr. Ferro, should I call for your car?"

Sean says, "No, thank you. Just taking my friend for a walk."

My heart beats harder. It's cold outside and I'm not dressed for it. I'm not supposed to leave the hotel. The little black bomb on my ankle will tell the ninjas to attack. After we pass the entrance, I dig in my heels and we stop. Sean looks at me with a strange expression on his face. I explain, "I can't leave the hotel grounds. She'll know."

Sean shakes his head and runs his fingers through his hair, grabbing at it. "This isn't turning out how I planned."

Although he seems to be talking to himself, I answer. "Nothing ever turns out the way I plan. It makes me wonder why I bother." Sean looks over at me. I grin sheepishly. "You caught me. It's not my life's ambition to be here tonight. I had other things planned, all of which got shot to hell. In a manner of speaking, you're my last chance... my last plan."

Sean seems surprised. His mood lightens a little. "Rule breaker," he teases. A light smile crosses his lips.

"Yup, rebel to the core." I answer. I sigh and suck in the cold night air and look around. People move up and down the street around us, all hurrying somewhere. I shiver and run my hands over my arms. "So, I can't pretend to understand your, uh, preferences, but if you want to swap me out—"

"No." Sean's eyes lock with mine. "You stay. I just have to figure things out."

"Why are we on the street?" I can't help it. I have to ask. I wrap my arms around my middle and try to keep warm. The wind blows gently, lifting the curls off my shoulders.

Sean looks at me. The expression says he can't tell me, and that something's tearing him up inside. His spine straightens and everything changes. "Listen, we need a new arrangement."

"Agreed."

"But I need somethings that came with the previous agreement. That's nonnegotiable."

"Fine," I say, shivering. "Let's go inside and discuss it like normal people."

"Since when are you normal? You run around with cans of ether in your pockets." He forgets himself and smiles. That hard mask he was wearing, cracks. My God, he looks beautiful.

The corners of my mouth lift. I step towards him. "Mind telling me why you were always at that corner?" I place a hand on his chest and smile up at him.

Sean shakes his head. "My secret." He's silent for a moment and adds, "You'll be safe with me, Avery, ah I mean, Miss Stanz."

Something flutters inside my heart when he says my name.

# 17

SEAN TAKES me to his room. It's the penthouse, located high above the city. The entire floor is ours. I've never seen such a place in person. Space is a commodity in the city and the vast size of the room is flaunting wealth.

"Do all guys get this room?" I ask, looking around. I feel Sean's eyes on me as I walk.

"I'd think not. It'd be a huge tip off. Plus the

room cost more than the average services your company provides."

My face flames red. I try to hide it, but Sean sees my blush. He walks toward me and takes my hands from my face.

I say, "I've not done this before."

"I know," he says, his voice deepening as he speaks. Sean keeps a hold on my hands and turns me from the window to meet his gaze. A light dusting of stubble lines his jaw. That dark hair that I want to touch so badly falls into his eyes. He tilts his head to the side and it falls back. "Tell me something. How is it that you're a virgin? I wouldn't have thought that could be possible."

My gaze darts away from his, but he tilts my chin so that I can't look away from him. My heart is pounding rapidly and I feel vulnerable. I want to jerk my face away. I want to run, but I don't.

His voice is a whisper, "Tell me."

"I never found the right guy," I breathe.

Sean's eyes devour me, raking over my face like he can't get enough. Finally, he nods slowly. His hands drop from my body and I feel nervous again. I'm nervous when he touches me and more anxious when he's not.

Sean sees the slight tremor of my hand. He

says over his shoulder, "I won't have sex with you, not unless you want it."

What? I nearly fall over. Did he really say that? "I'm sorry?"

Sean sits at a desk and turns the chair toward me. I stand in front of him staring with my lips parted. "It's the way I do things. I have no intention of forcing. Actually, the whole thing is left up to you, really."

I swallow hard and stare at him like he has two heads. "But, I thought..."

"I know what you thought, but that doesn't matter now. We need a new arrangement, since the old one won't work anymore."

"Why won't it work?" I don't understand what he's thinking.

"Because I know you. It just can't be the way I thought, so let's come up with something new. I won't lay a hand on you, unless you ask me to. I won't have sex with you unless you want it. How's that for starters?"

"Sean, I can't change things that much. It isn't right. You wanted something when you called for me. What did you want?"

He's quiet for a moment. The fingers on his hands lace together between his knees as he leans forward. I think he's going to answer me, but he doesn't. "Listen, this week is hard for me, okay? I'm not usually here, in fact I do everything I can to steer clear of New York at this time of year. Business didn't work out that way this year. I need something to occupy my thoughts when I'm not at work, someone to be with. Since I know you can do that on some level, I want you around."

When he speaks, I hear the hitch in his voice. Sean's running from something, something he doesn't want to remember and being here forces the memory forward. I nod slowly and walk toward him. "So the arrangement is platonic? Not sexual?"

"Yes, if that's what you want."

My heart sinks. I look at him and I have no idea what I want. I thought I was going to have sex tonight. I nod, like I'm in shock. My gaze is lost, staring somewhere across the room when he speaks.

"That isn't what you want, is it?"

"I—" my mouth hangs open and I have no idea what to say. I try to explain, but I can't.

Sean looks surprised. "You wanted to do it, didn't you?"

I shake my head, but Sean puts his hands on my waist and pulls me to him. "You're breaking your rule," I say.

"I don't care," he says with a dark look in his eyes.

"Okay, then."

"Tell me what you want from this, what you want to learn?"

"Learn?" I squeak.

"Yeah, I'm assuming you felt safe with me and wanted to learn something. Isn't that why you picked me from the file? I'm sure there's more than one guy with a virgin fetish."

My heart is pounding. I can barely focus. I nod, even though it's not the truth. "Teach me," I hear myself say, and wonder how much ether I've inhaled. I must have rotted my brain.

"Teach you what, Miss Smith?" He holds me close, warming me. His hands linger around my waist as his eyes hold my gaze. My heart beats harder, faster. My face warms as I think about his hands on me, about what he's offering me. I wish I knew what he wanted originally, but I don't. I look at his lips, wanting to taste them, wondering what it would be like to be with him.

Smiling shyly at him, I breathe, "Everything."

# 18

SEAN'S EYES are locked with mine. He doesn't react to my words. There's no smile on his lips, no sense of relief or joy. Instead, he stays a breath from my lips with his fingers gently brushing my cheek. His other hand is possessively holding me against his waist. His body is so hard. My thoughts keep drifting to running my tongue over his firm stomach. It makes my toes curl and I feel shy, but I don't look away from him.

No one has ever looked at me like this. I mean, it's not a gaze that's tender and sweet. Sean's eyes are filled with desire that darkens by the second. It's like his eyes could devour me whole. That carnal look makes my body grow warmer. My heart slams into my ribs like it's trying to save itself, like it knows Sean's bad for me.

I don't know what I expect Sean to do, but he's slow about doing it. He teases me, leaving his lips so close to mine that I tremble. By the time Sean closes the distance between us, I can barely control myself. He brushes his bottom lip against mine. The electricity that's been building between us ignites and I suck in startled breath. My legs feel like they want to run, but I can't. My muscles twitch like my fight or flight response is taking over, but I force the sensation back. There is no way Sean will hurt me. Miss Black made it clear that she'll hurt him if something happens to me. My heart, on the other hand, well, that's a different issue.

I stand there as Sean's body is pressed tighter to mine. Every curve, every muscle, slips into place until there is no space between us. His body is rock hard and so warm. I feel him under the supple fabric and know how much he wants me.

Sean's fingers gently tangle in my curls, as he brushes his lips past mine again. The floor of my stomach falls away and it feels like I'm falling. The kiss is so light, so perfect. It makes me lightheaded, like I'm drunk, and as soon as his mouth is gone, I want more. My eyes flutter open. I didn't realize that I'd closed them.

Sean pulls back and watches me with that intense gaze. It burns a trail between my eyes and my lips. Sean tilts his head in and rests his forehead against mine, locking our eyes. I feel his rib cage expand as he sucks in a jagged breath. Excitement is brimming beneath the surface, barely contained.

I don't know what I want or what I want him to do. My mind is lost in a cavern of lust and I can't find my way out. Hell, I don't even know if I want out. My life sucks and this little reprieve is heaven. There's no reason to think, nothing to worry about. After this tryst, I'll have what I need as well as plenty of memories to keep me warm on cold nights. So why am I trembling? What am I afraid of? I made peace with this decision. Yeah, keep telling yourself that, a bitter voice says at the back of my mind.

It takes me a moment, but I realize that Sean frightens me in a way that I can't fathom. Most of the fears in my life are tangible, but this one isn't. My emotions feel dazed, like they don't know what's real and what's fake. Sean doesn't really love me. I don't love him, but still—there's something there and it calls to me.

The way his eyes drink me in, the way his hands feel on my skin, and the way he teases makes me crazy—I've never reacted to a guy like this in my entire life. There was never any heat, not even a spark. That's what makes things with Sean all the more insane. From day one, I felt something for him. He walked into my life and filled a hole that I didn't even know was there. It's too soon for that. A couple of kisses and smiles later, and I sound like I'm ready to marry the guy. What the hell is wrong with me?

Sean watches me closely as I think. Every time I take a breath in, my breasts press harder against his chest. It feels right. I want more. As if he can read my mind, Sean lowers his lashes with his gaze fixated on my lips. When he lowers his mouth to meet mine, the thoughts rush from my mind. Like a surging river they race through, and are gone before I can blink.

Sean's fingers drift down to my cheek and he tilts my head to the side. My heart pounds harder in my chest. His lips are full and soft. They seek mine, applying the perfect amount of pressure and the kiss deepens. I push my body against his chest and my arms wrap around his neck. I play with the hair at the base of his neck as he kisses me, feeling the silky strands slip between my fingers.

As we kiss, a thought races through my mind, a warning. Something about kissing. It flutters through my mind, unclear. Sean licks the seam of my lips once, and then twice. My heart races harder as he does it. I'm ready to open my mouth and let him kiss me deeper. I want it. I want him. My body is charged, ready for that kiss. Every inch of me is tingling. There's a wave of desire building inside of me and his kiss will set it free.

His kiss. Kissing...

"I can't," I say into his mouth as the memory hits me. Gasping, I pull away and turn my face.

## 19

THE KISS BREAKS. I can barely breathe. The rapid pace of my heart won't slow. My hands tremble at his neck and there's no way to hide it. I pull away from him and cold air fills the space, chilling me. "I'm sorry."

Sean says nothing at first. He watches me. I feel his eyes slip over my body. They take in the slight tremor, the way I wrap my arms around my middle, and the way I can't look him in the eye.

Instead of demanding my services, Sean slips back into his chair like he doesn't mind. "There's nothing to apologize for."

I glance at him from over my shoulder. I don't believe him. My gaze says as much.

Sean smiles at me. "It's part of the package, Miss Smith. Skittish virgins are appealing." It's the look he gave me when my car broke down. Something about the way he gazes at me makes me feel like I'm in emotional overload.

My face flushes and I glance away. What was I thinking? I can't do this. I can't be with him, not when he affects me like this. The whole sex thing is a pastime to him, but to me it isn't. I took this job because I needed the money, but even more so, I took this job because I have feelings for Sean. I like the way he makes me feel. I want to know him better. I want him to be mine.

That's not what this is.

The trembling becomes more noticeable. Sean stands and walks up behind me, rubbing his hands over my arms. He presses a kiss to my temple and holds me. "Your preferences said kissing on the lips was off limits. I shouldn't have done it. I apologize."

"You went straight for the only thing you

couldn't have?" I did mark that on the sheet. Kissing forms attachments. I can't be attached to him. You already are, a voice says inside my head. Go to hell, I answer, already knowing it's true. I feel his gaze on the side of my face.

Holding me tightly, Sean says, "It's my nature. I'm sorry, Avery. It won't happen again, not unless you ask me to kiss you."

As he speaks, his warm breath breezes past my ear. I shiver in his arms and feel him smile. I nod. The knot in my throat makes it difficult to speak.

Sean holds me like that for a moment and then asks, "May I ask why that particular action is off limits?"

I feel him breathing against my back. Sean's pressed his body against my back and holds me tight. "Only if I can ask what you originally wanted this weekend." I glance at him.

"Ah, then it seems we are at an impasse." Those glittering blue eyes conceal his thoughts.

I nod. Damn straight. I'm not spilling my guts if he won't spill his.

Sean's voice is deep and rich. "I suspect the reason, but assumptions usually don't turn out well."

"Are you calling me an ass?" The corners of my mouth tug up. Seriously? What's with him?

Sean laughs like he has no idea what I'm talking about, and turns me towards him. "What?" The smile reaches his eyes.

"You know what happens when you assume, don't you?"

Cocking an eyebrow at me, he tilts his head and tuts, "Grade school humor? Really? Is that what this night has deteriorated into?" Sean shakes his head and sits back down, slumping back into the seat.

I shrug my shoulders and step toward him. "It might be different if you told me what you wanted. I might want that, too." I cross my ankles and gaze at him. Whatever plans he had for the night were blasted to bits when I walked through the door.

Darkness drifts across Sean's eyes, like he's remembering something that he wants to forget. It changes his confident stance and his shoulders slump a little bit. His chest tightens along with his throat. The muscles strain as he tries not to react. I didn't mean to do that to him. I know it's from what I said. I feel horrible about it and want to take away the pain in his eyes.

I walk toward him, not having a plan, just doing whatever feels right. "Sean," I say softly. When he doesn't look up, I put a hand on his shoulder. Still no reaction. I lift one leg gingerly and straddle his lap. That gets his attention. His eyes flick up to mine. A warning shoots through me, but I ignore it. There's something dangerous about him, I can sense it.

I'm standing over Sean and slowly lower myself until I'm on his lap, facing him. I rest my wrists at the back of his neck and look into his eyes.

Sean doesn't move. He doesn't say anything. I tangle my fingers in the curls at the base of his neck and lean in close. Heart pounding, I press my lips to his cheek. I repeat the action, and do it again and again, until I reach his neck. My stomach twists as the space between my legs grows hotter. I tilt my hips, and try to shift my weight on his lap, but Sean stops me.

Watching my face, Sean takes both of his hands and slips them under the hem of my dress. His hot palms run over the outsides of my thighs until they rest on the curve of my butt. Sean holds me tight, and pulls me higher onto his lap. That's when I feel his hard length through his pants. I gasp and dig my fingers into his shoulders.

Sean doesn't smile. Instead, I have the Sean from downstairs, the one who's all dark with no light in his eyes. His fingers press into my skin and he skims the edge of my lace panties.

Neither of us speaks. Sean watches me, always keeping his gaze on my lips as he tilts our hips making his erection rub against my thin panties. I can't hide how much I like it. Cupping my ass, he pulls me against him and then I push back. I'm writhing in his lap, my eyes locked with his. My body aches for his touch. I'm not satisfied with his hands on my bottom. I want them on my breasts; I want them all over me; inside me. I lean my head back and rock against him. Arching my back makes my breasts press against my bra. I moan out loud, and his name slips from my mouth.

That is the action that undoes him. Sean stands suddenly, taking me with him. "Wrap your legs around me," he says as he stands and walks across the room.

The spot between my legs is pressed against him as he walks us to the bed. His gaze doesn't change. The heat in his eyes says that he'll devour me. I wonder what he'll do. Sean leans me back on the bed and looks down at me. "Tell me what you want," he says, climbing onto the bed and laying next to me. His hand strokes my cheek.

"You," I say breathy, "I want to be with you."

Sean's eyes slip over my body after he pushes himself up onto his side. "Tell me when to stop."

I nod. Apprehension shoots through my veins, but lust is boiling hotter. Sean's hands are on me and my eyes close. My back arches into his hand, wanting to feel his touch. Sean starts at my neck, his finger slowly drawing a line down the side of my throat, across my collarbone, and between my breasts. The movement is painfully slow, teasing and igniting heat that surges through my body.

Lightly, his finger traces the swell of my breasts and circles back between them, stopping at my navel. Sean's finger dips in the small indent and continues down, over my dress, and doesn't stop. I gasp when that light touch reaches the dip between my legs. Sean's eyes are locked on mine as his finger trails between my thighs.

I can't look away from his face. I feel trapped, even though I know I can tell him to stop. Sean's hand returns to my face, and this time when Sean trails it down my neck, his fingers remain on my skin. The violet dress has a low neckline, and Sean dips his finger beneath the luxurious fabric, tracing the swell of my breast with his finger.

I breathe harder, wanting him there, wishing he'd do things to me that I never thought I'd want. My nipples harden and press against the lace bra. An image of Sean's teeth, gently tugging the sensitive skin flashes in my mind. I gasp and thrust my chest up toward him, but he doesn't touch me like that. Everything is light, like a snowflake touching skin. His other hand mirrors the movement, tracing the smooth flesh along my neck and down to my breast. By the time he's finished both sides, I'm writhing on the bed. Every bit of me is hot. I've never wanted a man so much. I don't know what to do. My instincts say to pull his lips to mine, but I can't.

Instead, I grab hold of his shirt and yank him toward me. I sit up off the bed and strip his shirt, fumbling the buttons one at a time until they come undone. Sean lets me undress him without saying a word. When I have his shirt off, I nearly die. Every inch of him is ripped, like movie-star-OMFG-ripped. The tanned skin is smooth and taut. Muscles rise and fall in perfection. Sean's body is Greek God material. I stare and reach for him, but Sean's hand darts out and he takes my wrist, stopping me.

Shaking his head, he says, "No touching."

Disappointment floods through me and I feel my bottom lip go into a full pout before I realize what I'm doing. "But, why?"

Sean smiles wickedly and leans toward me. His eyes fixate on my mouth. "Pull that lip back in right now or I swear to God, I'll kiss you so hard that you come."

His words shock me. My lip returns to its normal position, but the place between my legs throbs at his suggestion. My eyes lock with his and I feel the surprised, hopeful look fill my face. Heart racing hard, I say, "Can you really do that?"

My only answer is a wicked grin. Before I can say anything else, Sean sits me up. His hands reach for my sides and he starts to slowly unzip the dress. The way he watches me makes me feel excited and uneasy at the same time. I'm perfectly still, trying not to react. Even though I said no kisses, I can't stop looking at his mouth. Images flash through my mind of a kiss that could make me come.

Sean must see it on my face, because he smiles at me. "Just ask, Miss Smith."

I grin at him in return, as his hand slips inside the dress, feeling the smooth curve of my waist. "Don't hold your breath, Mr. Jones."

Mirth flashes in his eyes, and my dress disappears. I'm lying on the bed, propped up on my elbows in nothing but my lingerie. Sean is kneeling on the bed next to me. He drinks in my body like he can't get enough. First his eyes sear across my breasts, and then dip down to my waist, before his gaze lingers on my panties. I try to be calm and confident, the way Miss Black told me to behave, but I can't.

I smile at him shyly and look away. Something inside me wants to cover my body so he can't see me. Sean's finger resumes its slow tracing. When the pad of his index finger slips over my nipple, I can't stand it anymore. I grab him by the wrist. "If you don't touch me, and I mean take me in your arms and press your hands over every inch of my body, I'm going to scream."

Sean grins at me. He leans in close—his lips are next to my ear—and answers, "Will you scream my name, because I'd like to hear that." Before I can answer, Sean presses his lips to my throat, takes me in his arms, and lays me back on the bed. Sean's body is on top of mine. I feel his hard length pressing against me.

That hard body is all mine. My fingers rake down his back as he kisses my neck. The edges of my vision flicker. When I close my eyes, white bursts of light appear. The throbbing between my legs connects to every kiss. Slowly, my legs part and I want him there.

That's when the night goes to hell. In a matter of moments, everything goes from complete ecstasy to complete crap. I hear a high-pitched chirping sound coming from across the room. Sean looks up at the same time I do. Neither of us recognizes the sound.

Sean asks, "Is that your cell?"

Shaking my head, I answer, "No. My phone doesn't make that noise." And I have no idea what does.

Sean stands and leaves me lying on the bed. I turn on my side as he walks toward the windows, toward the noise. He presses his hands against the glass and looks down. "Fuck."

## 20

"WHAT IS IT?"

Before he can answer there is a knock at the door. Sean turns in time to see the door open, and drops the black box back into my purse.

Miss Black stands flanked between two large men. They're dresses like hotel patrons in expensive suits, like they might have come to the hotel for a business dinner. They must be the kickass ninjas that Mel mentioned.

Miss Black steps into the room. I take the bedspread in my hands and cover myself. "Mr. Ferro, I believe you're in violation of your contract." She doesn't even look at me when she steps across the threshold. "Get dressed Miss Stanz. You're leaving."

I don't understand what's happening. When I don't move, Miss Black waives a hand at one of the large bald men flanking her. The one with dark skin and inky eyes steps toward me. He picks up my dress from the floor and hands it to me. "Dress yourself, Miss Stanz, or I'll have him do it for you."

Sean leans against the ledge of the window frame with his arms folded over his chest. He looks pissed. "Mind telling me which rule was violated?"

"You know very well which rule, Mr. Ferro." Miss Black looks down at her dress, like she's looking for a piece of lint. She smoothes the skirt and glances at me as I pull my dress over my head. I have no idea what she's thinking, or what we did, but here she is.

"Humor me," Sean replies. The look in his eye says he's not happy. The muscle in his jaw works, while he waits.

Black looks him over, with her little brow pinched. "Very well. You took our property off premises. We don't do three strikes here, Mr. Ferro. You were careless and you know, as well as I do, what happens to careless clients in this business."

Sean walks toward her slowly, "I am well aware, however, the violation was an oversight. Miss Stanz followed me outside."

"Why would you do that?" Miss Black's gaze slips from Sean's to mine. I stare at her, heart racing, knowing that I'm going to be busted. Sean can get another virgin to screw, and I'll get kicked to the curb.

I open my mouth to confess, but Sean cuts me off. "Because I asked her to."

"Mr. Ferro, rules are set in stone. We cannot have clients disregarding them. The rules aren't guidelines, they are mandatory. I'm afraid that you'll need to seek your needs elsewhere." Miss Black snaps her fingers at me. "Come, Miss Stanz." Miss Black turns on her heel and walks through the door. I glance helplessly at Sean. He inclines his head slightly, telling me to go. I grab my purse and follow Miss Black out. The two large men are behind me.

Miss Black's long strides are quick. I hurry to keep up. "What happened?" I ask as the elevator doors close. We're alone.

She sighs, like she's annoyed. "He really told you to go outside?" I nod, sticking to the story. "She presses her manicured fingers to her temple. "Men like that are nothing but trouble, always pushing the limits to see how much they can get away with. I'm sorry for putting you through that, Avery. It won't happen again."

"I don't understand how you knew. We didn't go very far. And what was that beeping sound?"

"There's a transmitter in your bracelet." She glances at my wrist. "I already told you that. We know exactly where you are. Where is it?"

"I put it on my ankle." I point and it's still there. "It didn't fit around my wrist."

Miss Black acts like I'm a first grader. "Wrist, Avery—it has to be on your wrist. I'll have it resized." She shakes her head like I'm an idiot.

"I'm sorry. I didn't know."

"Well, you wouldn't. You just started. The beeping noise was a pager we put in your purse." She takes my bag and opens it, taking out a little black box. "It goes off when we are outside the building. That only happens if a client violates their contract. It lets you know that we're coming. I don't normally show up at all, but with you being new, I didn't think you'd leave willingly with the security personnel."

I nod and look at my purse, wondering when she put that inside. I thought I had my bag with me all night. Sean must have seen the pager in my purse when he walked over to the window. I wonder how he knew what it meant. Sean seemed to know that Miss Black was coming. "Has he done this before?"

Miss Black looks at me, confused. The elevator slows as we reach the ground floor. When the doors open, she resumes her hastened pace. Looking over her shoulder at me, she says, "No, not that I know of. He was a new client."

A car is waiting for us at the curb. Miss Black walks toward it with her head held high. A valet holds the door open for her and she slips into the car. I follow behind her. The men that had entered Sean's room with Miss Black are gone. I don't see them anywhere.

"Stop looking, dear. They're invisible when they need to be." Miss Black slinks back into the seat. Her brow is furrowed and her eyes are pressed closed. "How far did you get? Tell me that you're still a virgin, please." Miss Black looks straight ahead. I'm sitting next to her on the limo seat.

"We didn't get that far. And yes, I am." And I'm not happy about it either. Or maybe I am. I don't know. Tonight was nothing like I thought it would be.

"Good," Miss Black says relieved. "You will be paid for your services for this evening. Mr. Ferro was required to pay in advance for this evening. So, you don't need to worry about getting stiffed."

"Bad pun."

She laughs and looks at me. I'm staring straight ahead, shell-shocked. "You're an amusing girl."

"That's one word for it," I mutter. Glancing at her, I say, "I'm sorry. I feel a little nuts. I thought I was going to—"

She cuts me off. "I know. This job can be an emotional roller coaster. Don't worry though. It gets easier."

I doubt it, although I say nothing. We arrive back at Miss Black's. I step out of the limo. Before I can walk away, Miss Black says, "I'll find you another client by next weekend. This won't be for nothing. I promise. Come up and let's get this squared away."

I nod, and silently follow her upstairs. I'm paid an insane amount of money, in cash. It isn't anywhere near what I thought I'd be getting, but it is enough to get me through a few weeks, as long as nothing else goes wrong. I take my money and shove it in my purse and head to my car.

After I spray the engine, it starts right up. I drive back to the dorm shivering, with wintry wind blasting my face. I considered sealing the window with duct tape, but that'll look even more ghetto.

When I get inside the dorm, I bypass my room for the moment and go to find Mel. Her door is cracked. It's a little after midnight. I wrap my knuckles on the wooden door and push it open. "Mel? You here?"

Her roommate, Asia, is sitting on her bed talking on the phone. She shakes her head at me, shaking her short shiny black hair. "One sec," she says to the person on the phone. Raising her voice, Asia says to me, "Mel is working late tonight. She said she wouldn't be in until after 2:00 am."

I nod. "Thanks."

Flustered, I walk back to my room. If Amber barricaded the door, I'm going to kill her. I slip the key into the lock and twist. Surprisingly, the door opens. My shabby little room is empty. Thank God! As soon as I know that I'm alone, the tears come and they don't stop until I pass out on my bed.

## 21

THE NEXT MORNING SUCKS. Amber and Dennis are arguing. I cover my head with a pillow, but it still doesn't block them out. To top it off, she has the heat cranked up so high that I'm sweating. I get up and turn down the heater. Hiding under the blankets doesn't work when the room is 150 degrees.

"Don't touch that!" Amber snaps at me. "It's freezing in here."

"I'm melting, Amber. Leave it off for a while." I sound reasonable, but she makes a face at me. As soon as I walk away, Amber turns the thing back on.

She turns her anger on me. "You're such a bitch, Avery. You can't do whatever you want, whenever you want. I live here too!" Amber is seething, like she's justified. Dennis watches her, but his eyes flick to me when I explode.

I round on her, growling, with my hands balled into fists at my sides. "Are you fucking insane? I never get to do what I want! You're here all the time, you lock the door, you block me out of my own goddamn room, you have sex on my bed when I'm not here, your boyfriends use my blankets to clean up after they stick their dick in your nasty self! If anyone's a bitch, it's you!" Amber is staring at me, her eyes becoming glossy like she's going to cry. I don't care. I so don't care.

"You're so mean, Avery," Amber sobs and turns to Dennis, who holds her in his arms loosely.

Dennis listened to my little rant. It's quiet for a second before he asks her, "What did she mean, boyfriends?" He emphasizes the plural part of the word. "I thought we were exclusive, Amber.

Have you been fucking other guys?" He pulls her away and shouts in her face.

I'm so angry. I grab my clothes and run out the door. As it slams behind me, I hear Amber sobbing, saying nasty stuff about me, denying that she was with anyone else. I don't know why he would care. Dennis screws any girl that lifts her skirt. Enraged, I walk down to Mel's and knock. It's still early.

The door creaks open and she looks at me with bleary eyes, "Awh, hell. You want me to go punch Tramperella in the face? Cuz I'll be all over that piece of trash. You just say the word. I could hear you guys screaming from here." Mel yawns the last part and glances down the hall. When I don't answer, she blinks hard and pushes past me. "I'm gonna go all ninja on her white ass. You come on and watch."

I grab Mel's arm and stop her. "Maybe later." Mel looks at me and then back down the hall. I coax her. "Let me use your shower and I'll take you out for breakfast."

Mel gives me a look that's distinctly Mel. It's all attitude. "I want chocolate chip pancakes, and not that shit the diner serves. Are we talking IHOP?"

I laugh. "Yeah, if that's what it takes."

# 22

BRIBERY IS UNDERRATED. I think I could get Amber whacked if I bribed Mel with a stack of chocolate chip pancakes. She eats them, doused in strawberry syrup. The pancakes look like they've been shot.

"How can you eat that?" I ask. It's so sweet. I have eggs and bacon. Well, I had bacon. Mel took that already.

"It's freakin' fantabulous. Everyone should

eat this for breakfast. Every day. It's the breakfast of champions." She shovels another bunch of fluffy pancakes into her mouth. A bead of syrup runs from the corner of her mouth.

"That's Wheaties. And you're looking a little vampy, there." I touch to corner of my mouth and tilt my head toward her and say, "You've got syrup. Or is that drool?"

Mel's back stiffens as she wipes away the blot of red. She points a fork full of pancakes at me and says, "I do not drool. Not unless it's a particularly hot guy. Then I might drool, a little." She chews and takes a swig of milk, then asks, "So, how'd last night go? Are we still on Team V?"

I laugh. "You're so stupid. Team V. Yeah, I'm still on Team V. Things got out of hand last night. Black showed up and pulled me away."

Mel's jaw drops and the fork freezes half way to her mouth. "No shit!" She leans in closer and lowers her voice, "What the hell happened?"

I tell her. As I retell the horrible events of last night, I push around the food on my plate. I don't feel very hungry today. When I finish my story, I look up at her. Mel hasn't taken a bite. I tell her, "Black said she'd match me to someone else. I got paid a little bit, enough to treat you and pay some bills, but not enough to be home free the way I thought I'd be. I don't know what to do."

"You're back to square one."

I nod. "Yeah, I suppose so."

"Why did Sean do that? It almost seems like he wanted to blow the whole arrangement."

"He didn't. He didn't react well when I showed up. He left. I chased him. It's not like he lured me outside to irritate Black. He seemed as surprised as I was when she showed up."

"That boy is messed up." She points her pancake at me before popping it into her mouth.

"We already knew that." I sigh and lean my head on my hand. I poke my eggs and paint the yellow yolk across the white plate.

Mel watches me. "You seem out of it. If I didn't know better, I'd think you were falling for the guy. You're all doe-eyed, making hearts in your food."

"I am not," I say, straightening up.

"Whatever," Mel says, "I just call it like I see it. You've got that Bambi look on your face, like you're swooning for Mr. Freakshow."

I snort-laugh. "You're so mental. That's not it. I just don't know if can do it again."

"It's just one guy, one time," she reminds me.

I nod. "That's what it was supposed to be this time."

---

AFTER BREAKFAST, I head to the library to get caught up on school work. The building is huge and smells like dust and old paper. Once I get into the stacks, the lighting sucks. I navigate my way through the massive building until I find my little chair in the corner. It's a good spot because no one ever comes back here. There's a desk and chair against the wall at the end of one of the rows. I toss my book bag on it and pull out my work.

After a few hours pass, I'm leaning with my hand in my hair, staring at the cinderblock wall in front of me. I can't concentrate. I have no idea what to do. I thought my financial problems were solved and that I could go back to studying. Sean was ideal bait, but then Black sent him packing. I don't know if I can do it with someone else.

Memories flit through my mind and I can feel Sean's hands on my skin. I wish Black hadn't shown up. I wish things progressed further. I wonder what it would feel like to have my sweat-covered body slip over his, what he would feel like inside of me. My body warms at the thought.

I'm so out of it that I don't hear Marty until he's next to me. "Well, look what we have here."

I jump out of my skin when he speaks and twist in my chair. I had no idea he was there. Marty laughs at me. He's wearing a pair of dark jeans with frayed patches on the thighs, coupled with a tee shirt and denim jacket. His blonde hair is spiked. He looks like an 80's remnant.

I swat at Marty, meaning to slap his leg, but he dodges my hand. "You scared me to death!" I whisper yell at him.

He laughs and drops his backpack on the floor next to my desk, and then takes his extra tall body and leans against the wall. Shoving his hands in his pockets, he says, "Only people with something to hide get all skittish like that. What'd you do? Kiss a girl?" He winks at me and grins.

I cover my heart with my hand, willing it to resume a normal pace, but it ignores me. I don't look at Marty when he speaks and he catches on. "So, you do have something to hide. Is it juicy?" I glance at him, thinking that direct eye contact will help, but the guy sees right through me. In a hushed voice, he squeals, "Oh my God! You have to tell me!" As Marty talks, he falls to his knees and scoots toward me, clutching his hands under his chin, like he's begging.

I laugh it off. "There's nothing to tell." I squirm in my chair and go back to reading my textbook.

"You're a bad liar."

Sighing, I say, "I know," and slump forward, planting my face in the book. "I can't lie, but I can't tell you."

He grabs my shoulder and pulls me up. I look him in the face as he asks, excitedly, "Is this about the questions you asked the other day?" My face must answer for me, because Marty gets more excited. "Oh my God, you did something morally deplorable, didn't you? What was it?"

When I don't answer, he starts reasoning it out, which scares me to death. He ticks off his fingers, "Well, we both know it's nothing to do with lying. So that leaves cheating," he ticks off a second finger and pauses, looking at my slumped shoulders, and says, "Yeah, I can't see that one either. You're hardwired to not cheat. That leaves stealing, adultery—"

"Are you just going to list the seven deadly sins and hope I confess when you hit mine?"

He waves a finger in my face. "Ah ha! That means it was one of the big seven."

"You're an ass. Leave me alone." I pretend to read my book. Marty grabs the pages and yanks it away. "Hey!"

"You tell me everything, why can't you tell me this?" he says holding my book just out of reach. I make a grab for it and miss. He's too damn tall.

"Because I can't. And it doesn't matter now anyway, because everything is all fucked up." I stop jumping for my book and sit down hard in the chair. It feels like a wave of hopelessness crashes into me. Suddenly, I can't breathe and my heart is pounding. I grab the hair on the sides of my head and look at the floor, saying, "I can't do this." My breathing becomes labored, like I'm having an asthma attack.

Marty puts my books down and kneels next to me, placing his hand on my back. "Whoa, Avery. Calm down. Slow your breathing."

Tears well up behind my eyes, but they won't fall. For once, I wish they would. I wish I could just cry and have this part of my life over with. I rock in the seat. "I can't do this."

"Do what, honey? Be more specific." Marty's hand rubs small circles on my back. He leans closer to me. "Tell me, love. I'll help you however I can."

"But that's just it," I look up at him with glassy eyes. "You can't help me, no one can. I have to do something that I don't want to do. I'm fucked every way 'til Tuesday with no way out."

Marty keeps his hand on my shoulder and looks at me with an expression that I can't read. It's not pity, it's something else, more like pity's bastard cousin. "Avery, you ever think that you're alone because you want to be?" I bristle at the suggestion, but he presses a finger to my lips to shut me up, and shakes his head. "No, don't talk. Listen. There's a time for listening, and that's now. I know you've got no one and that you're all by yourself, but you don't have to be. I'm here and so is Mel. You shut us out, Avery. When things get hard, you retreat into yourself and no one can get through those walls you put up. It doesn't have to be that way. Friends are your family now. I know that I'd do anything for you, you don't even have to ask."

Awh, fuck. His words trigger the tears and they rush down my face. Marty smiles at me, like he knows better. Maybe he does. Maybe I'm the one who's fucked up. Maybe I don't have to do everything by myself, but I don't know what that world looks like. The only people that I could depend on through thick and thin were my parents. Family was everything to them, to me. Now that I don't have one, I feel lost, like I don't belong anywhere, like I can't fully trust anyone.

I wipe the tears from my face with the back of my hand.

Marty reaches into his pocket and hands me a clean, white hanky. It's perfectly folded into quarters and creased like he ironed it. He holds it out to me.

I laugh, half choking on the phlegm in my throat. I take the hanky and dab my eyes before wiping my nose. "You made me cry. No one makes me cry."

"Really?" he asks wryly. "Everything makes me cry. Why do you think I walk around with a hanky?" He grins at me.

I look down at the white cloth in my hands, damp with tears. The confession spills out of my mouth. "I was offered a position as a high dollar call girl. If I take it, it solves my money problems. I can finish school and move on with my life."

"But..." he prompts, assuming nothing. Marty's great like that. He doesn't condemn me.

"But the obvious. But I'd be selling my body. But I'd be letting some stranger have sex with me. But, I'd be giving away my virginity to some freak..." my voice fades as I say the word, thinking of Sean.

Marty smiles softly and adds, "But you like someone else."

I look up at him. "How'd you know?"

He shrugs, "Just a hunch. Something about the way your voice sounds, like there's more there than you're saying. So who is this guy?"

I look at my hands as I speak. "No one. I don't even know. He helped me when my car got jacked. I've seen him a few times, and then I got the job offer. After talking to you the other day, I took it... I took the job because he was the client. Then, things got messed up, and now I can't have him." My voice hitches in my throat as I speak. Shaking my head, I ask, "What's wrong with me? How can I like a guy who's that twisted? He ordered a virgin call girl."

"And you showed up," Marty says, patting

my knee. "Listen, life doesn't always make sense. Maybe this whole thing's fate, maybe you're supposed to be with this guy in the end—I don't know—but it seems to me that's what's holding you back."

"What is?"

"That fucked up guy. You're totally sure that there is no way for him to be a client again?"

My eyes flick to his. I shake my head. "No, the madam was really pissed."

"Then, raise the stakes. Tell her that it's him or nothing."

"And what if she says no?" I'm screwed if she says no.

"Then, you're no worse off than you are now. Why not try to get the money and the man? Go for the gold, girlie. You're only young once." He bumps his shoulder into mine and smiles at me.

"Got any more clichés that you're dying to use?"

"Nah, I just know how much they irritate you. Go find your boss, call girl. And if you work things out, I'm taking you shopping." Marty gets a giddy look in his eye. "I saw this perfect little dress at Black Label. Any guy would love to rip it right off of you."

I laugh and lean into his shoulder. The hole in the center of my chest, that painful ache that was consuming me, withers and I feel like maybe I can do this. I have to convince Miss Black to get Sean back. I can do that.

I think.

## 23

AFTER PROMISING Marty that we'd go shopping tonight, I head to my car. Pulling the seat forward, I toss my books in the back. When I go to push the seat back, it won't move. It's not as cold today, but still—standing in a parking lot alone is asking for trouble. My track record for getting robbed is shamefully high. I yank the seat, but it's stuck. I climb in the backseat and put all my weight into it and pull, trying to force it into an upright position. There's a cracking sound and then seat comes free and falls back into place. I try to squeeze between the seat and the door so that it doesn't get stuck again, but I don't fit. So, I'm forced to climb through the bucket seats, head first, and I pretty much fall out the door. I stand, brush myself off, and jump into the car. I lean back before grabbing the seatbelt. The crappy old seat holds. I half expected it to snap off.

I start my decrepit car and head toward Miss Black's. When I arrive, the place is bustling with people. I've never seen anyone here before. There are workers at desks. I hear a woman talking on a phone saying something about insurance for employees. Shocked, I stand there in the doorway to the office with my mouth hanging open. It takes this many people to run a brothel? The phones ring nonstop. It's like the call girl call center.

Miss Black spots me from across the room. She's standing at an aged man's desk, handing him a file. An irritated look flashes in her eyes and she quickly walks toward me in her tailored suit. She tucks the remaining files under her arm. "May I help you?"

Nodding, I look at her. "Yes, I believe so."

"Very well, come with me." Miss Black has perfect posture, even in those heels. She walks in front of me and I follow her back to her office, where she closes the door. "It is extremely unprofessional to arrive unannounced, Avery."

"I'm sorry," I say taking a chair. I sit on the edge of my seat and place my hands on her desk. Miss Black is leaning back in her seat, legs crossed. "I needed to discuss something with you."

"I'll allow it this time, however, in the future, if you want to speak with me, it has to wait until you check in on the weekend."

"That's just it. Since things got messed up the other night, I wouldn't be checking in and I didn't want to wait for you to call me. I decided that I'm not cut out for this." My heart is pounding as I speak. I try so hard to keep my nerves off my face. My hands rest perfectly still on her desk. There is no tremor in my voice. "I'm withdrawing my application. Thank you." I stand, like I'm going to walk away.

Her little speech about what a rare commodity I am is my only card to play. I'm totally bluffing. I need this job, but I want it on my terms. I step towards the door and reach for the knob. Miss Black doesn't say anything until I'm ready to pull the door open.

"Wait," she says. I stop and turn to look at her. "Please sit." Miss Black straightens in her chair and leans forward, her eyes tracking me as I walk back toward her and sit down. "The other night was an anomaly. That is not the usual course of events. In all my time doing this, that is only the second time I've had to intervene. I apologize that it made you question your choice to work here. There are other clients who have been on our roster longer, that have a proven track record. I would—"

I cut her off, "I'm not interested. The thing is, I didn't feel threatened the other night and while it might have broken your rules, he didn't make me feel like a prostitute. I didn't expect that to happen. I was the idiot who followed him outside. He wasn't the one who broke the rule. I did."

Miss Black looks at me with her dark eyes. The tips of her fingers press together one by one as she watches me from behind her desk. "You're not telling me something. What is it?"

"I'll consider staying, if I am given a second

chance with that client. I won't leave the hotel this time. I'll do my job, and you'll get your money." My throat tightens as I speak. My heart is racing so fast. This scares the hell out of me. The whole thing, and here I am telling her what to do. For all I know, she has those beefcake ninjas locked in her closet and they'll bust out and break my face for suggesting such a thing.

Miss Black stares at me. I don't breathe. My tongue is between my teeth to keep me from spewing her with nervous chatter. Her index fingers press together and then she taps them three times, like she's deciding something. "So, this is about money?"

No. "Yes."

"And…" she prompts.

"And I didn't think I could do this, but after the other night, I know I could follow through with him."

"Even if I wanted to, I don't think I could get him back. We exchanged some terse words after the event." Miss Black taps her desk. She glances up at me.

My words rush out, "Just tell him. If he refuses, then I'll consider someone else. Are we agreed?"

Miss Black isn't stupid. She leans toward me and says, "Something else is going on here, of that I'm certain. However, I'm not one to blow a business deal over suspicion. I'll ask him, under the condition that if he says no, that you'll continue working for us—that you'll trust my judgment when I select another match for you."

I didn't want this part. I suck at lying. I can't just yes her, she'll see it in my eyes. My stomach twists as I extend my hand toward her. "Deal," I say, and we shake on it.

I agreed to be with another man if Sean won't have me.

I hope to God that he says yes.

# 24

"NO FREAKIN' way is she wearing that dress,"
Marty says with his hands folded over his chest.
He towers over Mel, who is sitting next to him in
the middle of a swank shop. Either way, I need a
dress for my next tryst. I'm still waiting to hear
back if it will be with Sean or not. My stomach is
twisting in knots. I don't feel like shopping, but I
hope it will distract me. Since Mel and Marty

disagree on everything, it's been an interesting evening.

"How can you say that?" Mel says exasperated. This is the seventh dress, the seventh pair of shoes, the seventh set of accessories that I've put on over the last hour and a half. "Look at how tiny her waist looks in that thing. That is THE dress."

Marty gets up and stands next to me. I'm on a little riser, standing in front of a mirror. The shop attendant looks at me, but says nothing. Marty points to my hips, "True enough, but it does nothing for this region and her boobs! My God, she looks like she's nursed sixteen children. The braless look is for girls with falsies, not our Avery." Marty gestures at my cleavage in this dress, or lack thereof. I look down. Okay, maybe he's right. "A good dress doesn't sacrifice one asset for another." He snaps his fingers at the attendant. "Next, please!"

"You're such a drama queen," I say as I step off the box. I add, "And stop snapping at the girl like she's a labradoodle. She hates you enough already."

He bats his eyes at her. "Sorry love. I just get

so excited. You're doing a smashing job. Keep up the good work."

The attendant, Amanda, smiles and nods, but I'm sure she's picturing strangling Marty in her mind. "I'll get the next dress you chose. Just leave that one in the dressing room for me and I'll put it back."

I nod and traipse into the dressing room. I unzip the dress and pull the supple fabric over my head before putting it back on the hanger. I'm standing in my undies when my phone buzzes. I wouldn't have heard it if I wasn't in the dressing room. I pick it up and recognize the number. It's Miss Black. Immediately, my heart starts to pound and hope fills my chest.

"Hello?" I say, answering the phone with a swipe of my finger. I'm so excited, so terrified. I want the perfect dress for Sean. I can't wait to hear when our next date will be. Sean made it sound like we'd be seeing a lot of each other.

"Miss Stanz, good evening." Miss Black sounds the same as usual. It's hard to read her emotions. Maybe she doesn't have any. "I've contacted Mr. Ferro and wanted to call and tell you the results of our conversation. As I suspected, he is no longer interested in using our services."

A rush of air leaves my lungs and I sit down hard on the puffy seat inside my dressing room. "You told him that it'd be me?"

"Yes, I did. He was rather adamant that he no longer wishes to pursue the arrangement with you, even after I told him that you requested we call to correct this situation. I'll find you another match. Give me a little time and we'll have you all set. I'll call you when everything is ready. Have a good evening." And then the line goes dead. I stare at my phone. I feel like a hollowed out pumpkin. I put my head between my hands and try to collect myself.

Black's words bounce around in my mind. In a few moments I realize what they mean—Sean doesn't want me. He rejected me. Worry pinches my face as I wonder what I did. Why would he say no? The other night, everything seemed perfect. I don't understand why he would do this. I thought he liked me.

There's a knock on my door. Amanda's voice makes me jump. "I have your next selection here." She opens the door and hangs the dress on a hook. When she turns to look at me, her smile falls. "Are you all right? You look ill."

"I'm fine," I manage to choke out. Pushing away the feelings bombarding me, I plan to fake my way through the rest of the night. I hand her the dress that made me look flat and pull this one on. It's deep blue with silver stitching along the hem. There's a thin belt at the waist and a neckline that dips into a deep V. The skirt hugs my hips before it flares at the thigh. It's sexy and cute, all in one dress.

Zombie-like, I wander into the center of the store and show the dress. There's a fake smile plastered on my face. Mel and Marty both gasp when I walk out. It's a good sign.

Marty speaks first, "That is the dress, like the fuck-me-three-ways-til-Tuesday dress."

Amanda blinks, like she's never heard a crass word before.

"Will you shut up, Fifty Shades of Gay, and let her show us the dress!" Mel says to Marty, and hops up to look at me. "Spin around, honey. Show off your stuff." I turn slowly, palms raised while they look me over. "You look hot, Avery. I agree with the drama queen over there. You have to get this one. It's perfect. Sean will love it."

I swallow hard and keep the smile on my face. "It's not for Sean."

"What?" they say in unison.

Marty looks at Amanda and flicks his hand while he talks, "Go get us sparkling waters, honey." Amanda smiles and walks off. No doubt she's going to spit in his. Marty and Mel flank me. We look in the mirror as we talk in hushed voices. "What happened? How do you know?"

"I got a call while I was in the dressing room. Sean declined."

Mel's eyes go wide and she looks at Marty who is uncharacteristically silent. Mel takes over. She slips her hand around my waist and says, "To hell with him, then. You don't need him, Avery. He was eye candy. A crush. Nothing more. I'll help you pick out a new guy, someone better."

Marty eyes her. "You too? Is the whole school whoring, now?"

Mel goes on the defense. She folds her arms over her chest and narrows her eyes. "You got a problem with that?"

"No," Marty says, almost whining, "I feel left out."

That makes me laugh. It caught Mel off guard too and she snorts so loud that she sounds like a pig. We both stare at her. "Like you expected him to say that?" I shake my head. "Where'd you find this basket of gay, anyway?"

"He's my lab partner," I respond, waiting to see what Marty does about the gay accusation, but he just glosses over it. I wonder what's going through his head. The last time I assumed I knew something about someone from the way they looked, well, it didn't go well. It turns out that the woman wasn't pregnant. Since then, I don't blurt things out like that.

"That was witty," Marty says, pressing his hand to his chin and examining Mel like he's never seen her before. "I like what you did there." The two of them chatter and I look at the dark blue dress knowing that some other guy will be taking it off of me. I swallow hard and walk back to the dressing room to take it off. This is the dress that will be on me when I solve my financial problems. This is the dress that some guy will remove from me the night I lose my virginity.

Several hundred dollars later, I'm leaving the swank little shop with a new dress and silk shoes. It cost a good chunk of the money I earned with

Sean, but it's necessary to do whoever's next. After we walk outside, I put the things in my car.

"Let's go grab a bite to eat," Marty says.

"Sounds good to me," Mel replies.

Marty claps like he's five and yells, "Shotgun!" This is a major turn of events, since he rode to the store with me. Mel met up with us and brought her car. Glancing at me he says, "No offense hun, but your car scares the glitter out of me."

"None taken," I say. "Listen, I'm going to run an errand and head back. I'm not really hungry, yet. Late lunch." I'm lying, but neither one calls me on it. I wave and duck into my car.

I have to pick up my last paycheck from my previous employer. By the time I get there, it's dark outside. The sun sets so early at this time of year. My sweater doesn't do much to keep the chill away. I need to buy a coat. My mother would have yelled at me for wearing something so thin. God, I miss her. On chilly nights like this, she'd be cooking chicken noodle soup. Bread would have been baking in the oven all day, filling the house with that wonderful aroma. Memories like that sneak up on me at the worst times. I sit in my car for a moment, trying to push the past away.

Moving fast, I jog across the parking lot and walk into the front of the restaurant. There's a line of people waiting to be seated. A man is talking to the hostess. There's a beautiful woman on his arm. She has deep brown hair with a hint of red. A black dress clings to her curvy body. I envy her for a moment, wishing that I had curves like that.

"Hey, Stacy," I say as I approach the hostess. "I just need to pick up my check."

"Sure, but they weren't ready when I came in. You might have to wait for it."

I nod, intending to walk past her. I'm dressed like a bum, with tight jeans and my holey sweater. I stand out like a stripper in a preschool. A chill washes over me as I'm about to pass her. The guy at the podium turns. His blue eyes lock with mine and I freeze in place.

Sean.

We stare at each other for half a beat. Sean's wearing a black suit that fits him so well. It shows off his shoulders and his trim frame. The shirt he's wearing is the color of the night sky, perfectly blue—dark like my new dress. A chill encases my heart, as it tries to climb up my throat. I can't do anything but stare.

The girl on his arm, leans in close, possessively. "Is there a problem?" she snaps.

I blink and shake my head. I hate her. I hate everything about her. I want to rip her face off. My fingers flex at my sides as I think about it, but I'd rather Sean didn't know how hung up I am on him. "No ma'am," I say, knowing ma'am pisses off anyone under thirty years old. "Your table will be ready in a moment."

I shoulder my way past them, leaving Sean staring after me.

I get to the back room and find Lenny's office. He's my boss, or he was until Miss Black stole me away. "Hey," I say, my heart still racing from seeing Sean. "Is my check ready?"

"Yeah. I just finished. Here it is. I hope you come back, if you ever need a job again. You're a good kid." Lenny hands me my check. He's an older guy with gray stubble on his face. His white hair is thin and flops to one side. He reminds me of my dad when he isn't screaming at the staff.

I nod, fingering the check. "I will. Thanks for everything."

"No problem, Avery."

I smile at him and leave the office. I head through the kitchen and get enough dirty looks to last a lifetime, but I have to get to the back door. There is no way I'm leaving through the front. I'm lucky I maintained my composure the first time. If I see Sean again, I'll go nuts.

I leave through the receiving door and walk around the parking lot, back to my car. The parking lot is well lit, but there are still patches of shadow. I eye my car and hurry, walking fast, rubbing my arms to try and keep warm. A jacket is definitely a priority. When I get to my car, I stuff my check in the glove box and grab a can of ether. I lift the hood and hold it up while I spray, holding my breath so that I don't breathe it in.

"Miss Smith," a familiar voice says behind me.

# 25

"IT'S a wonderful night for a spray-start car," Sean says. Startled, I flinch and the can of ether goes flying. It smacks into my windshield, chipping it, before rolling down into the engine. Sean reaches under the hood and grabs the can. "A bit jumpy, are we?"

"Yes, I am," I say, snatching the can from him, after I drop the hood. "When strange guys come up to me, things never end well." I try to walk past him to get in my car, but he doesn't move. When I look up into his face, I'm angry. "Better get back to your new hooker. She didn't seem like a patient woman, if you ask me."

"I didn't ask you," he says with confidence that I've never felt.

"Real nice. You scared the crap out of me and cracked my windshield. Unless you plan on robbing me, go away." I fold my arms over my chest and look anywhere but at Sean. The parking lot is fairly empty. It's dinnertime and the place is packed. It's always packed.

"What would I take? That dress you have in the backseat—"

"Tell me what you want or go away," I say. My nails are biting through my sweater and into my skin. I lock my jaw, trying so hard to keep from saying something stupid.

"Is that dress for your next lover?"

"It's not for you, if that's what you're asking." I'm bristling. I don't mean to. I don't want to, but I can't stop. Sean has my blood pumping and my body just reacts.

Sean's eyes flick over me, like he's amused. "I don't wear dresses, although I appreciate the thought."

"Let me in my car," I hiss and drop my hands to my sides. He's blocking the door.

"What will you do if I say no?" His eyes sparkle, like he thinks this is funny.

I lean in close to his face. A twisted smile snakes across my lips as I speak. "I'll take your nuts off and then run you over with my car."

Sean flinches and steps away from the door. I push past him, brushing his shoulder and fighting the urge to throw myself into his arms. I'm so messed up. He's on a date with a hooker and I still want him. How many times was I dropped on my head as a baby? There's no way that this is normal. I sit down hard in the driver's seat and yank the door shut.

Sean leans on the door, resting his hands on the roof. He speaks into the open window. "You're beautiful when you're angry."

"Go to hell." I turn the key in the ignition and the car backfires and rumbles to life. God, could this be worse? Is he here to taunt me? I don't get it. I throw the car into reverse and rev the engine, ready to peel out, but his words stop me.

"I would have rather had you." Sean straightens and turns to walk away. His hands are in his pockets as he strolls back toward the restaurant.

The car sputters and stalls. I stopped feeding the engine gas without realizing it. I throw the car into park and jump out. "Wait!" Sean stops and turns around to look at me. There's a golden glow on his head from the light above. His hands are in his pockets and there's a faint smile on his lips.

I leave my car where it is and run the three steps toward him. "What do you mean?"

Sean looks me over like I inhaled too many fumes. "You are my preference."

I stare at him like I've been hit in the head with a board. "Then why did you tell Miss Black no?"

Something flashes behind his eyes, but it fades quickly. He tries to conceal it by looking down and pushing a rock with his shoe. "I shouldn't have," he confesses.

"Then fix it." Heart beating too hard, I stare at him.

Sean's gaze lifts and meets mine. "I am under the impression that it's not the kind of thing that I can fix."

"If you don't want me, I suppose I can screw

someone else—" I turn from Sean, but he grabs my wrist and pulls me back.

"I never said I don't want you." He flips open his phone and dials. I stare at him. Someone picks up. "I've changed my mind," he says without any introduction. "Yes, Miss Stanz. I want her delivered to my doorstep wearing nothing but a bow tomorrow night." He hangs up before the person can respond. His eyes are locked on mine the entire time. "Is that plain enough?"

Giddy hope flutters inside of me. I'm so fucked up. Why do I like this guy? He's on a date with a hooker. He ordered me on the phone. He wants me naked, in a bow.

"Maybe." I try to hide my smile, but suck at it. I rub my arms, trying to chase away the chill.

Sean takes off his jacket and places it over my shoulders. "Come inside and have dinner with us."

All sorts of nervous energy snake through me. I twist my hands and say, "With you and your hooker? I'm not into threesomes. I know it's not on my list yet, but I'm pretty sure I'm not into that."

"How do you know if you haven't tried?" His voice is light, teasing. He grins at me.

"Because I'm possessive. I don't share."

Sean looks down and then up again. The movement makes my stomach feel like it's floating away with my brains. Those dark lashes are delicious. "I like that. I don't share, either. The woman is my accountant. We were going over some records this evening. I didn't think I'd see you again, but I'm glad I did. Come inside."

I shake my head and look back at my car. It's halfway out of the parking spot. "I can't. I mean, I shouldn't. Black would be pissed if she found out about it." And you act so hot and cold, that I feel like I have whiplash.

The way his eyes devour me makes me weak. Somehow Sean manages to get close to me. Before I know it, Sean's rubbing his finger over my arm, gently. He looks at me from under his lashes, and says, "Please."

I melt. How can I refuse him? He sees it in my face. I offer up one last halfhearted protest. "But, I'm not dressed for it."

He takes my hand, "I don't care." Sean pulls me to his chest and wraps his arms around me. The way he looks down at me makes me shiver.

Desire flames to life inside of me. "I wish I could kiss you." His lips barely brush mine as he speaks. It's a cruel trick, a kiss without kissing.

"Maybe, someday."

This makes him smile.

# 26

I SIT at the table in my tattered jeans and oversized sweater, feeling out of place. When I look up from my plate, Sean's eyes are on me. He explained to his accountant that I was an old friend and that I'd be joining them for dinner. Her eyes sweep over me before giving me a look that says she thinks I'm no threat. Whatever. She can take her perfect body and shove it. Besides, all Sean's attentions are directed at me.

Dayla has a tablet on the table, where she presses buttons, asking Sean to clarify expenses. "You can't take a deduction on that Sean."

"I wouldn't have come here if the damn merger went through." Sean says, ripping off a piece of bread from the loaf on the table. "The additional trip isn't an expense?"

She sighs, "Your private jet isn't an expense. I need the fuel bill when you get back, along with these other papers." Her eyes flick to me. "Can you believe him? He avoids New York at all costs and then spends money like it's water when he finally gets here."

I have no idea who Sean is, why he's avoiding New York, or the reason for the sudden spending spree. I just smile politely and say, "Yeah, Sean's always pissed away money like a drunk sailor when he hits the Big Apple."

Sean grins at me. Dayla rolls her eyes. "It wouldn't be so bad if he told me what some of these expenses were. Like this one. What cost you $8,000 last weekend?"

Sean's eyes remain amusedly locked on mine. My stomach flutters. "Entertainment," he says.

It takes me a moment, but I realize what he spent that money on. That was the down payment for me. Sean sees the comprehension in my eyes and winks at me, while Dayla has her eyes glued to her tablet. Excitement flutters through me and I smile awkwardly.

Dayla looks up and says, "I need more information, Sean. Honestly, how am I supposed to be your accountant if you don't tell me specifics? I need specifics." She glances at me, looking for help.

I lean back in my chair and say, "I'm not getting involved. He's your client. You fix him."

She laughs lightly and gives me an "if only" look. "God bless the woman that brings him to his senses."

Sean doesn't look phased, but his eyes shift between us, like it worries him. He cuts our conversation short. "Unless there are more questions, we need to be on our way."

"Nothing you didn't already avoid telling me." Her pretty face pinches as she scrolls through her tablet, shaking her head.

Sean stands and says, "Do the best you can. I don't expect you to find a way to deduct, claim, or mark everything as an expense." She nods slowly, like her mind is still reeling from the meeting. "Please, take your time. I'll take care of the bill."

"Email me a copy," she insists. "This was a working meal."

Sean nods and heads to the front. I don't know why I didn't see him when I was working here. I would have remembered him. "Do you come here a lot?" I ask.

"No, why?" He tells the hostess that he'd like to settle his bill with the waiter. She rushes off to find him. Sean turns back to me, waiting for an answer.

"I worked here, until a few days ago."

He grins at me. "You got a better job, I hear. One with benefits."

I laugh, "Benefits for you, maybe."

"Miss Smith, you dismiss me too quickly. I assure you this arrangement will benefit both parties." The hostess returns with our waiter. Sean's eyes rake over me, openly admiring my body. I look away, unable to process what's happening. We just had dinner. That's all. We ate. Pull yourself together, Stanz.

Sean settles the bill and gives the waiter a big enough tip to render him speechless. His jaw drops as Sean walks away with me on his arm.

The nippy night air blasts me in the face as soon as we're outside. I shiver and try to race toward my car, but Sean grabs my wrist. "Where do you think you're going?"

"Home, lunatic. I'm not supposed to be with you right now."

"Says who?"

"Says you," I say to him, smiling. He's wrapped his arms around my waist and pulls me to him. I mimic his phone call from earlier, "I want her delivered to my doorstep wearing nothing but a bow."

Sean smiles. The way it spreads across his face makes me melt. Oh my god. "I did say that, didn't I?" I nod. "Well, we haven't had dessert."

I twist out of his arms, laughing lightly. "I am not eating dessert with you."

"Who said we'd be eating? You're the dessert," Sean says tugging my arm playfully. "And I can't wait to taste you."

I can't wipe the smile off my face. Laughing, I pull away from him again. "I have to leave. Go eat a Kit Kat." He follows me across the parking lot to my car. I stop in front of my door, expecting him to try and kiss me, but he doesn't. Sean remains two steps away. "Thanks for dinner."

"My pleasure." There's a look in his eye. It makes me want to be chased.

I open my car door and grab the can of ether. I spray the engine, walk back to my seat, slip in and close the door. Sean is sitting next to me in the passenger seat. "So, dessert."

"Seriously?" I laugh. "This is the car from hell, or have you forgotten?"

"Oh, I have not forgotten. This car is vividly seared into my memory." Sean takes my hand and lifts it to his mouth and presses his lips gently. A light tugging sensation snakes through my body, pulling me toward those lips like they're magnetic. Sean lifts his sapphire eyes and looks at me.

I forget to breathe. I forget everything. I take a jagged breath and pull my hand from his. "I need to go."

"I'm going with you." Sean takes his seat belt and pulls it across his lap, ready to shove it into place.

"I wouldn't do that."

# 27

HE DOES IT ANYWAY. The metal clicks and his seatbelt is buckled. "Tell me not to come if you don't want to see me." Sean watches my face as he says it, knowing that I don't want him to leave. He lifts his hand to my face and trails his fingers down my cheek. Images of slippery bodies pass through my mind.

"That's not it." I breathe. He's an inch from my lips. That tugging consumes me. I want to close the distance and press my mouth to his, but I don't.

"Then what is it?" he replies softly.

I'm quiet for a moment. I've forgotten what I'm talking about. His eyes are so beautiful. The curve of those lips is hypnotic. No wonder I can't think around him. I find my brain and tell him, "That seat belt only buckles. It's doesn't unbuckle."

Sean grins wolfishly, like he just deflowered an entire flock of virgins and I'm next. "I guess I'm going with you, then."

Shaking my head at his tenacity, I start the car. It lurches out of the parking spot and I get onto the road. Sean reaches for the heater. I tell him not to, but it's too late. A puff of white smoke shoots out of the vents. Reaching for the switch, I flip it off. "Don't touch anything."

"There's no heater?" he balks, but when he glances at me, he looks concerned. "Why aren't you ever wearing a coat?"

"Because I don't have one. They're expensive and it seemed like a waste of money. When it's really cold out, I have a sweater I can wear."

"You mean that other oversized ball of yarn I saw you wearing?" I nod. His eyes flick to the window, where it's cracked open next to my head, blasting me with cold air. "Why are you still driving this thing? It's a death trap."

I shoot him an evil look. "Seriously? You're asking me why I'm driving a shitty car? Because, I don't have eight grand to blow whenever I want. I can barely keep this thing running as it is." There must be something about the way I say it, because Sean doesn't press me. Instead the topic shifts to him.

Sean's fingers are at the top of the window, and he looks outside and up at the sky. "I haven't been here at this time of year in a long time. I forgot how much I like it. The air smells like snow." He gives me a half smile and asks, "Where are we going?"

"You'll see." I drive into a park. It's past dark and there aren't many lights along the road once we're inside.

Sean looks around and says, "If I wasn't stuck in my seat, I'd be worried you were going to hack me up and leave me in the woods."

Grinning, I reply, "I have to get you out of the seatbelt somehow."

"You're a little twisted, you know that?"

"Oh, and you aren't?"

"I never said that." Sean gives me a look and shakes his head.

"What then?" I say, driving past the building I was looking for. There are a few cars in the parking lot. I drive around back and stop the car. It shudders and dies.

"You surprise me, that's all." Sean looks around and asks, "Where are we?"

"At the skating rink." I get out of the car and walk around to his side. I yank open the door to find him trying to free himself from the seat. "I'll get it. Wait a second." I flip open the glove box and grab a screwdriver. I lean across his lap and shove the screwdriver into the buckle. I can feel Sean's breath on my cheek. His scent fills my head as I jiggle the screwdriver and the buckle comes free. "There." Sean's gaze is intense, like I just did something so sexy he's going to die. The way he looks at me, makes every nerve in my body feel like it's strung tight. I want to scream in giddy excitement and laugh.

"Thanks," Sean says, his voice a little too husky. I turn and walk away from the car. Sean steps out of the old car and slams the door. "What are we—?" he asks but doesn't have a chance to finish before getting hit in the face with a snowball.

I laugh hysterically, standing next to the enormous pile of ice shavings from the rink. After they fix the ice, all the shavings are dumped out back to melt. It's the funniest thing to grab some snow and hurl a snowball at someone when it's summer. Since it's cold outside, there is a lot more than normal because it hasn't melted yet, but still—Sean doesn't expect it. The look on his face is priceless.

Sean turns toward me in slow motion, his eyes taking in the pile of snow. "You took me here to have a snowball fight?"

I nod. "Well, I can't exactly take my chastity belt off for just anyone. You have to earn it, man."

"I thought I bought it," he says, walking slowly toward the pile of snow. It's taller than both of us. It looks like the huge snow piles you see in parking lots after the plows push all the snow aside.

I back up the hill, grinning like a lunatic. "You bought the belt, not the key."

"I'm going to pretend that I'm not in metaphorical hell and—"

Smack! I hurl another snowball at him. It hits his cheek and explodes into powder.

"You talk too much," I giggle and start grabbing snow and throwing snowballs as fast as I can.

Sean doesn't hesitate. He runs up the pile of snow in his black suit and tailored black coat. He runs up the hill so that he's higher than me. I nail him in the stomach with a few throws before he has time to retaliate. A snowball clips my ear and the snow goes down my sweater. My hands start to sting from my lack of gloves, but I don't really notice. We're laughing and jumping around on the snow hill, pegging each other like little kids. Sean laughs so much that his eyes water. When I least expect it, he charges me running straight at me. Sean's body collides with mine, and he pins me in the snow, holding my hands down at my sides.

I yelp as snow goes places it shouldn't. "You suck! Let me go! Lemme go! Lemmegahhhh!" My laughter turns into hysterical screeches when he yanks my feet and snow gets shoved up my back. I try to twist away, but he doesn't let me.

Flailing, I kick my legs out of his grip and swing. My leg clotheslines him and Sean falls next to me. I take my chance and jump on top of him, straddling him and shove snow in his face. "You're so mean!" I laugh, trying to make him eat snow.

Sean grabs my wrists and pulls me down on top of him. Our eyes lock and I can't look away. I'm freezing, but I don't care. I want him. Leaning in slowly, I think about kissing him, about how it would feel. That's when someone opens the backdoor to the ice rink and starts yelling.

"You damn kids! Get the hell out of here!" He can't see us, it's so dark, but we've been so loud up until now that he knows we're here. He shines a flashlight at the snow pile.

My eyes go wide and I stifle a laugh. I get off Sean and pull him to his feet, dragging him by the wrist around to the back of the snow pile. We stay there for a second, until the guy gives up, and then burst out laughing.

"Holy shit," he says, doubled over and breathing hard. "I haven't gotten yelled at like that since high school."

"Yeah, what'd you do then?" I say, laughing.

"Toilet papered the principal's car... and got caught by said principal when he left for lunch early." Sean snorts a blast of laughter and shakes his head. "He let me have it."

I smile at him as we head to my car. It feels like I should take his hand in mine, but I don't. We smile at each other and get back into the car. Breathing hard, I look at him. My face is frozen and I've been smiling so much that it's stuck like that.

"Thanks," I say.

"For what?" Sean looks at me, but he doesn't know it yet. There's a stain that mars my life. It hangs over me like a lead balloon.

"I haven't laughed so much in a really long time."

Sean takes my hand and holds it to his lips, cradling my frozen fingers between his. "Neither have I." Sean opens his mouth, like he wants to say more, but he doesn't. Instead he releases my hand and I drive him back to the restaurant where he grabs his bike and we part ways.

# 28

BY THE TIME I get home, I'm cold and tired. My head is spinning, unable to understand how tonight went from disastrous, to bliss. The laugh lines on my face seem like they're going to be etched onto my skin until I walk into my dorm room. Amber is on top of some guy, riding him like a horse, and they're both naked. I look away, but it's not before I get an eye full of her bouncing boobs and sex noises that I could have lived without hearing. Again.

I go into the shower and lock the door. I stay in there forever, hoping they'll both pull their groin muscles or something. After a while, the hot water beats on my back and I start thinking about Sean. I wonder if I'll ever be like that. Amber's a skank. I wonder what made her that way, and hope to God that it doesn't happen to me. When I get out of the shower, I wrap myself in a towel and pad out into our room. The monkey loving is over, and I head to find clothes.

Amber is sitting up on her bed with a pink sheet draped over her body. The guy she was with is gone. Disgusted, I say, "Was that the fourth guy this week?"

"Yes, no thanks to you. Dennis tried to dump me after you blabbed." Amber grabs a pack of cigarettes and smacks them into her palm after opening the window. She's smoking again. Wonderful.

"There'd be nothing to keep secret if you didn't screw every guy who walked in here." I yank a pair of sweats on and head to my bed.

Amber laughs bitterly, "You need to get laid.

You should have taken up what's-his-face up on the three way."

"You disgust me," I say, staring at the ceiling and wishing she'd fall out the window.

"Are you saving yourself, Avery? You think the right guy will just waltz into your life and you'll be in love? Get real. Life doesn't work that way. Sex is dirty. It has nothing to do with love."

"I feel sorry for you," I mutter, not thinking about what I've said.

"Screw you, bitch. You act like you're better than me, but you're not. You're a goddamn whore, you just don't know it yet." She sucks on her cigarette and holds it in. "Or maybe you do and that's why you're such a bitch." She releases a cloud of white smoke out the window.

When people find out that Amber's my roommate, they feel sorry for me. Her reputation precedes her. She's a total whore and everyone knows. The thing is, while she's absolutely vile, her words are true. I turn my back on her and feel the center of my chest cramp. After tomorrow, I'll be a whore—a real one.

Pressing my lips together, I say, "You're right."

Amber laughs, like she doesn't believe me.

She waits for me to say something else, to bash her again, but I don't. I can't. I'm a hypocrite. I don't like that she's slutty, because it affects me. No, that's not true. I don't like her because she's vile, because she's always got some guy's dick in her mouth. At least, that's what I've told myself all this time.

I don't want to think about it anymore. I close my eyes, willing sleep to come, but it doesn't. I lay there long after Amber passes out. My heart races so hard that I can't stand it. I curl into a ball and feel the tears streak my face. I wish things weren't the way they are. I fall asleep, wishing my life to be different, hoping for a miracle.

# 29

MISS BLACK CALLS me and lets me know that I have a date this evening. I wear my new dress. This time I change in my room. Amber isn't around. She's avoiding me, which is kind of nice. I zip my new dress and put my heels in my shoulder bag, since I have to drive my car to Black's.

When I arrive, Miss Black looks me over, approves my dress and then does all the measurements. Lastly, she comments on my lingerie. I'm wearing a white cotton set that's trimmed with embroidery and lace. The bra is no more than a shelf. It barely conceals my nipples. If I lean forward, I'll fall out of the bra and the dress.

Miss Black says, "The bikini panty is fine for the virgin gig, but when this is over, I want you in a thong or g-string. No exceptions." I feel like a bad employee. I nod and don't say anything. She seems to think that I'll be staying here for a while, even though I told her that I'm not.

"Since the other night didn't go well, I'm changing protocol with you. Here's a phone. I will call you if your bracelet goes off premises. Mr. Ferro gets no more chances, understood?" I nod and she shoos me. "Get dressed and go to the car, and remember—confidence. Even if you have no idea what he wants or what you're doing, act like you do."

I walk to the car that's waiting for me at the curb and climb into the backseat. I've had more time to think about this, so I'm not as nervous. Last time I was near puking. This time I just have a serious case of butterflies. The car pulls up in front of the same hotel. I'm given the same room number, which surprises me. I wonder if this is his room, if this is where he's staying while he's in New York.

Shoulders back, I walk across the lobby to the elevator. I press the button to the penthouse. When the doors open I walk to the end of the hall and knock. Sean pulls the door open. He's wearing a white button down shirt that's open at the neck with a tie that's been undone. The shirt is tucked in at the waist to a pair of tailored slacks. He's barefoot. The stubble on his cheeks makes him sexier than he already is. His eyes slip over me and it feels like a caress.

"I told them naked with a bow, Miss Smith. Do I need to call your employer?" Sean sounds serious, but the smile on his face makes my nerves fade.

I walk past him and into the room. "They said I wasn't allowed to walk naked through the lobby."

"And you do everything you're told?"

"Only sometimes. Maybe." I smile. "I'll try it next time, if you like."

He laughs to himself and shuts the door. Sean walks across the room and closes a laptop that's open on the table. He's been working.

There are dark circles under his eyes like he's under a tremendous amount of stress. I didn't notice them last night. I walk further into the room and look around. It's the same as the other night. He must be living here.

Sean crosses the room and grabs a bottle from the bar. "A drink, Miss Smith?"

"No, thank you, Mr. Jones. I'm a professional. We don't drink."

"You're not allowed to drink, are you?" he asks.

"I can. It's not forbidden." He walks toward me with a predatory look in his eye. It makes my stomach twist.

"Then, why not?"

"I don't my first time to be when I'm too drunk to remember. Call me romantic, but it sounds more appealing to me that way." I'm nervous. My fingers tug at the fingers on my other hand. I try to stop, but then I just do something else.

Sean's eyes remain fixed on my cleavage. "You're very appealing, so is your notion of remembering." His eyes lift to my face. "Are you expecting to be interrupted this evening?" I shake my head. "Good. Let's begin where we left off last time. Strip. Throw that beautiful dress on the floor and lay on my bed."

My heart is pounding. I didn't think he'd do this. Sean's acting cold, distant. It's like I don't know him. "Are you sure?"

"Yes," he says evenly. "Do it." Sean sits down in the chair and watches me.

My heart is pounding so fast that I can't hide how nervous I am. Maybe I should have taken that drink. I reach for the zipper and slide it down. I shimmy my shoulders out of the dress and it falls to the floor in a puddle, around my ankles. Sean's hot gaze drinks in my body. When I turn away to walk over to the bed, he stops me.

"Wait." I stop. "Come here." I walk toward him with my heels still on. The bra barely contains me. I stop in front of him.

Sean reaches for me slowly. He places his hands around my back and pulls me closer, and then palms my breasts through the bra. The shock of how he behaves makes me want to cry. He's acting like I'm an object. I don't like this, but I can't stop. Sean doesn't get another chance. And if I say no, this is over.

Sean squeezes my breasts, but it scares me. It

doesn't feel like I'm here with him. I have a darker version of the man I lo—

Oh my God. That's when I realize it. I love him. I'm here thinking that this job is going to be something else, but it's not. Sean doesn't have any romantic inclinations toward me. I want to yell at him. I want to slap him in the face and ask how he could behave this way, but I can't.

Sean's eyes cut to mine and for a brief second, I see remorse. It's there and gone faster than I can blink. Sean is cold, detached. He points to the bed. "Go lay down, the way you were the other day." I want him, but I want the guy from the restaurant, the guy from the snowball fight, the one who stopped to help me get my car back. For some reason he's shut down and I don't know how to draw him out. Half way to the bed, I stop and look back at him.

"Do what I tell you," he says.

Heart pounding, I go to the bed and lay in the spot I was in the other day. He watches me, but doesn't move from the chair. "Spread your legs." I do as he says, parting them. My heart thumps wildly in my chest. I don't know if I can do this. I want Sean. I want to crack that shell.

"Now slip your hand down your panties and rub, slowly."

I glance at him, feeling shame spreading across my face. "Sean, please..."

"When you've done that, I'll come over." He doesn't move. The stern expression on his face doesn't change.

I can leave or stay. I can protest. Or I can do what he wants. Feeling foolish, I do as he asks. I slip my hand between my legs and rub. At first the only thing I feel is complete foolishness, but my body comes to life. I'm too emotionally charged for nothing to happen. Sean watches me from across the room. Slowly, I relax and just think about the sensations shooting through me. When I stop looking for him, Sean's next to me. I feel his weight on the bed.

Sean breathes in my ear. "May I?" he asks, slipping his hand on top of mine, lowering it to the sensitive flesh between my legs. I nod and go to pull my hand away, but he holds it there. "You stay," he says as he dips his hand lower and strokes my slick skin. I gasp, surprised at the intensity of the touch. My hips rise up to meet his hand.

My heart is beating so fast, so hard. I feel

warm and afraid. I want to relax. I want to be with him, but I'm not his lover. I'm his hooker. Before I realize it, tears are streaking down my cheeks. Sean's hand gently strokes me, but I don't look at him. I can't.

Sean's fingers slip inside of me and I jump. He's been kissing my neck and finally pulls back to look at me. "Avery," he says, his voice filled with concern. Sean takes his hand out of my panties and pulls me to his chest. Cradling me in his arms, he asks, "Why are you crying?"

Shaking my head, I say, "I'm fine. Something got in my eye." Sean nods and takes my wrist, pulling me off the bed. "Where are we going?"

"I want to take a bath with you. Can we do that?" his eyes meet mine, and although I don't understand, I do as he asks.

Nodding, I say, "Yes, that would be nice." I press my lips together and manage to stop the tears.

Sean fills the huge tub in the bathroom and invites me in. The room is blush colored marble, with white accents. It's beautiful. Sean takes my hand and pulls me to him. Wiping the moisture from my cheeks with his hands, he pulls me to him and holds on tight. He whispers in my ear,

"I'm sorry. I didn't mean to..." he sighs and pulls back, looking at me. Smiling sadly before glancing at the tub, Sean waves his hand, like I should step in clothed. I nod and step into the warm water. When I sit back, he takes my hand.

Sean smiles at me, but I still feel sick. I must look green because he says, "We don't have to do this."

"Yes, we do. I have to get over it and just do it. Nothing in my life turned out the way I thought it would. Why would this be any different?" I sound bitter. I can't hide it.

Sean sits on the edge of the tub and looks down at me. My white panty set is see through. When his gaze flicks back to my face, he says, "I'm sorry. I didn't mean to look before you're ready, but you're beautiful. I couldn't help myself."

I manage a weak smile. "You weren't acting like yourself." It's a statement, a fact.

His eyes dart to the side, like he's ashamed. "I didn't know how to act."

"I thought you've done this before."

"I have, it's just. This is different," he says, pushing his hands through his hair.

"Why? I don't understand."

"I know you don't Avery. Just believe me when I tell you that it's different. I didn't know the others. I know you. I like you. It changes everything." His voice drops to a whisper and he won't look at me.

I swallow hard, and stand in the water. Water pours off me in sheets as I stand and reach around to unhook my bra. The clasp comes undone and I drop it on the bathroom floor at Sean's feet. He watches me, his eyes darkening by the moment. He looks at my breasts like he wants to lick them. I shimmy out of the wet panties and toss them to him. Sean catches them. A smile flicks across his face.

"A sudden case of exhibitionism, Miss Smith?" he can't seem to pull his gaze up to my face.

I take his hand and pull him to me. His feet are on one side of the tub. I press my naked, wet body against him and drag my fingers through his hair. I decide that I have to do this all the way or not at all. I'm holding back and so is he. I hope that removing my barrier will cause his to come down as well.

Looking into his eyes, I say, "Shut up and kiss me."

# 30

ANY REMAINING wall that Sean has up, crumbles and falls. He presses his body tightly against mine before sweeping his lips over mine. The kiss is gentle at first and then becomes more demanding. His tongue sweeps over my lips, demanding that I part them. When I open my mouth, he dips inside. Sean kisses me harder and I love it. My fingers tangle in his hair. The damp shirt clings to his chiseled chest. I press my breasts harder against him, wishing that I could feel his skin against mine. As if he can read my mind, Sean pulls away and strips his shirt off. When he takes me in his arms again, our bodies are plastered together. My breasts smash against his hard chest. The ache in my nipples feels better when I rub against him. I writhe in his arms, sliding my body against his. Sean's hands trail down my back and cup my butt. He pulls me to him and lifts me out of the water. I wrap my legs around his waist and he carries me to the bed.

Looking into my eyes, he lays me back. "Tell me when to stop. I want you to like this, too."

I nod. My entire body is hypersensitive and craving his touch. As soon as his chest slips against me, I want his hands in places hands shouldn't go. My legs fall apart and Sean slips his fingers between them. He strokes me gently as he kisses me, finally slipping his finger inside of me. I push my hips into his hand, wanting more.

Sean pulls away, smiling and says, "Easy. Go slow. I don't want to hurt you."

I nod and lock eyes with him. I don't feel scared anymore. I just want him. I want to show him how he makes me feel when he looks at me with those sad eyes. I want to make him smile and I don't want it to stop. Taking his face between my hands, I pull him back down to my mouth. His hand slips between my thighs again and he presses inside me.

"Slowly," he says, pushing harder until I feel something pinch. I make a noise. It hurt a little, but I'm so turned on that I barely felt it. Sean stills his hand. "Are you all right?"

I nod and wiggle my hips against his hand. "Please," is the only coherent thought I have. My hips rock into his hand over and over again. A steady heat is building inside of me. If I don't have him inside me soon, I'll scream. Sean watches my body move as his hand turns me wanton. I manage to open my eyes and beg again, "Please."

It's like something inside him snaps. Sean moves and his hand is gone. I gasp, wanting it back. In a second, Sean is naked and on top of me. He strokes my hair away from my face and looks into my eyes. I feel his hard length pressing against my stomach. I want him between my legs. My mind is all lust. I tilt my hips against him, pressing into his leg.

"Are you sure you want this?" he asks.

I nod and suddenly feel like talking. I clutch at him, trying to pull him to me. "Please, Sean... please," I say, followed by a swarm of verbalized dirty wishes. I can't shut up. I know I'd never say anything like the stuff that's coming out of my mouth. I say dirtier things, things I didn't think I'd ever want before Sean placates me. His knee pushes my legs apart and he settles on top of me. One hand is on either side of my head, holding him up. I look at his spectacular body and have the impulse to lick it.

Sean says, "You're beautiful." I feel his dick between my legs. It rubs against me, making me crazy. I wrap my legs around his hips and push into him. He slides inside of me and I gasp. Sean stills as I get used to the feeling. "Are you okay?"

I nod. "Yes." Looking into his eyes, I put my hands on his ass and begin to rock. I do whatever my body tells me to, and right now it wants him deeper. I rock against him, wiggling my hips slowly, allowing the delicious sensations to overtake me completely. I have no idea who I am or what's happened to me. I forget all the pain that plagues my soul on a daily basis and lose myself in him.

Sean lowers his body on top of mine and

begins to push in, then pulls out slowly, and pushes in again. The movement is so charged that I can't take it. I dig my nails into his back and rock violently against him. Sean pushes into me harder and faster. The feeling inside of my core grows hotter and wetter, finally exploding, sending surges through me. I cry out as I come, my nails clawing his back. Sean keeps rocking into me, drawing out the feeling. Every part of my body is sensitive. I feel everything. There's a throbbing inside of me. It grabs hold of his hard dick and fills me with happiness. A moment later, I feel him throbbing inside me. Innocently, I ask, "Did you come?"

He nods. "Did I hurt you? I wasn't going to, not this time, but oh my god—you're so sexy. I couldn't help myself."

I smile at him and push the dark hair away from his eyes. "I liked it."

"I'm glad." Sean pulls out of me slowly and I moan. I reach for him with a smile on my face. "Come back."

He smiles at me and kisses me on the forehead. "I'm not done with you, yet. I'm going to get you Advil and warm up that bath water. Are you up for a little sex in the water?"

THE ARRANGEMENT

"That sounds perfect." I lay naked on the bed when he goes to get me a painkiller. I take it and drink the bottle of water he hands me.

When Sean comes back, he walks toward me completely naked. This is the first time I've gotten to really look at him. His body is ripped, with perfectly sculpted muscles in his legs, arms, and chest. And his abs, oh my God, they're so tight, so perfect. The compulsion to lick them shoots through me again. My eyes drift lower, and I don't conceal my lust. I stare at his erection as he walks toward me, and press my thighs together hard to try and control myself.

"What's that look?" Sean asks, stopping before me. I'm lying on my back, on the bed with the sheets immodestly draped across my body. My hair is fanned around my face in long dark curls. His eyes slip over me and that warm feeling returns.

I smile lazily. It feels like I'm floating on a cloud. "I feel fluffy, like I could float away."

"You're happy, then?"

I nod, still smiling like nothing could pull me down from this high. Before I can say another word, Sean scoops me up in his arms. I don't expect it, so I yelp and giggle until I'm secure against his chest. His skin is so warm and smooth.

I press the spot along his shoulder, tracing my finger over his muscle as he walks me to the tub. "I want to run my tongue over this spot."

That makes him smile. Sean glances down at me in his arms. He steps into the marble bathroom and stops. He doesn't put my down. Looking into my eyes, he asks, "Is there anywhere else that little tongue of yours wants to go."

A mad blush turns my cheeks red. I don't know where it came from or why it happened. I bury my face in his shoulder, trying to hide. He laughs, "Apparently, so."

He steps over the side of the massive tub with me in his arms. I cling to Sean, hoping he's more surefooted than me. I would have slipped. Sean plants both feet in the bottom of the tub and lowers me into the water, before sitting down himself. The tub is large enough to be a small pool. If I lay down, I could float and still have room before bumping into the walls. Sean sits opposite me and presses the button for the jets. He takes my hand with the bracelet and lowers it into the water.

"When I first saw you running down the side

of the road, chasing your car, I never dreamed I'd end up doing this with you." His eyes are hungry again, like he can't get enough of me. "What did you think of me?"

I look at the froth on top of the water and say, "I thought you were hot and that I don't have time for things like this. If someone told me that I'd be in bed with you tonight, I would have laughed my head off."

The thing is, I don't feel like laughing. I'm a call girl. This isn't real. This isn't what I wanted. I did what I had to do and was lucky enough to get him for a client.

WHEN I LIFT MY GAZE, it's like Sean can tell that shame is choking me. It's the first time since we had sex that I can really think clearly. That happy feeling has dissipated and all that's left is doubt. My stomach twists and I can't look at him.

Sean seems to sense it. He moves across the tub and takes me in his arms, kissing my temple after he does it. I lie against him for a moment and feel safe. How fucked up am I? This man won't protect me. He bought me. He's as screwed up as I am. Sean holds me close.

His voice is perfect, rich and caring, "Don't think about anything, right now." His hands grip the back of my head and he massages my scalp. It makes my brain slow. The thoughts that are flooding through my mind disappear when he pulls me onto his lap. At first, my legs are off to the side.

Sean holds me, stroking my head and doesn't let go. His other hand holds my back, tracing the curve as it disappears below the waterline. I stare at the wall, not thinking, just breathing. My head is against his chest listening to the sound of his heart. It comforts me. I don't think about what I've done. I pretend this is a date. I pretend that the affection between us is two-directional, that I'm not the only one who feels something. It's easier that way. I know that when I go back to the dorm, guilt is going to crash into me hard. I try to steel myself, but some things are impossible. There's no way to brace my heart for something like this, something that feels real but is no more substantial than vapor.

My throat tightens as I think. My body must tense, because Sean whispers in my ear, "Miss

Smith, I don't know if you're aware of this or not, but you are a very beautiful woman and I'm lucky to have you as my lover."

I can't help it. I smile against his chest. I decide to stop thinking. I'll follow my instincts. I finally cave into my obsession with his shoulders. I trace my finger along that spot—that perfect spot that I want to nibble. I press a kiss to his chest, over his heart. Sean stiffens, but I don't notice. I don't see the look in his eye, the way the pain shoots beneath the surface.

I'm too distracted. I trail the kisses to his neck, and shift so that I'm straddling him, kneeling over his lap so that I can slide my tongue along his shoulder. When I do it, my body flames to life again and any lingering thoughts are lost beneath a wave of desire. My breasts press into him as I lick his skin. Since we are both wet, his skin is slick and they slide as I rise out of the water to reach his shoulders.

Sean tilts his head to the side and moans my name as I do it. I trace my tongue over the rise and fall of his muscles, slowly licking and kissing his smooth skin. Sean's hands travel down my back and he cups my butt gently. Desire is building inside of me again. I slide my breasts against him, tracing the lines of his shoulders, pressing my lips to his damp skin. When I move to settle onto his lap, he's hard. Looking into his eyes, I slowly lower myself onto him. He's so hard and sharp. The sensations that shoot through me as I do it are divine. The soreness doesn't prevent me from taking him all the way in. If anything, it reminds me of that cloud of lust that filled my mind from last time I came. Sean's gaze remains locked with mine. He gasps as I take him in, his hands still on the curve of my hips, guiding me.

Neither of us says anything. I sit upright on his lap and Sean leans back against the side of the tub. His gaze lingers on my breasts before returning to my face. "You're beautiful, Avery."

I smile, because I don't know what to say. I never thought I was anything, and here I have a gorgeous man telling me that I'm stunning. Before I can think about it, Sean shifts beneath me. I gasp and my mouth falls open into a little O.

"You like that?" he asks and I nod. I liked that very much. Before I have a chance to ask Sean what he's doing, he does it again. This time I moan loudly and toss my head back. Sean grabs my arms so I don't fall backward. Breathing hard, he moves his hips in a slow circle. It puts pressure in all the right spots. My back arches and I scream this time. It feels like he's doing more, and maybe he is, but I'm not going to stop him to ask.

Sean remains perfectly composed, his eyes filled with fire as I climb closer and closer to ecstasy on his lap. He continues the movement, pressing his hips harder against mine, pushing me closer to the edge. I can barely hold myself up. I have no idea where to put my hands. Before I can think about it, they're on top of my head, tugging at my hair. I don't think about how I look or what he sees. I just enjoy what he's doing to me. My breasts ache for his touch, but Sean keeps his hands below the water, tightly gripping my ass. The world goes fuzzy and the only thing I'm aware of is how I feel, how Sean makes me want him. Heat builds within me, making me hot even though we're in the water. As Sean moves inside me, it's all I can do to sit up.

When he says, "Come for me, Avery," he thrusts his hips against mine and I can't control myself. I feel the pulsating from deep within me and ride him as hard as I can. Water sloshes out of the tub as I do it. My hands are on Sean's shoulders as I thrust harder and harder. He watches me with a carnal look on his face. His eyes move between my bouncing breasts and my face; his hands hold me tight to his lap, pushing harder, deeper. I shatter and fall against his chest, breathless. Sean's hands find my damp hair. He kisses the side of my face as a whirlwind of pleasure shoots through my body. He's still hard inside me, which makes the aftershocks more delicious.

I barely come back to myself as he starts kissing my neck. I still can't speak. I'm a mess of heat and jagged breath. I feel his warm lips press gently against my hot skin. One of his hands is in my hair, the other around my waist. He lifts me off of him, making me gasp, and settles me on his lap and holds me, so that I'm facing away from him. I lean into his back and he wraps his legs around my hips. His arms wrap around me and he holds on tight, like I might fly away.

We sit there in silence for a long time. I wonder what he's thinking. When we get out of the tub, Sean takes me to the shower. He grabs my hand and we step into the steaming shower stall. Using shower gel, Sean rubs his hands over my body and soaps me up. Next he uses the shampoo and works it into my hair. Then, he turns me around and pulls my body against his, before the soap is rinsed away. With one arm wrapped around my chest and the other around my waist, he holds me tight. I turn my head to the side and let him hold me. Sean doesn't let go right away. I notice that his heart races, but I don't know why. It pounds wildly, like he's running or afraid. Taking his hands I loosen his grip and turn back toward him.

"What's wrong?" I can't ignore it any more. Something's bothering him. I have no right to ask, but I want to make it better.

Sean smiles sadly at me and says, "Nothing." That's the end of the conversation. We rinse off and get out. Sean hands me a fluffy white robe. I slip into it, and thank him. He nods and leaves me to untangle my hair in the bathroom.

It takes me longer than I wanted, but I don't have conditioner or the stuff I use in my hair. Combing it felt more like pulling it out. When I emerge from the bathroom, Sean is dressed. He's wearing his clothes from earlier, with one exception—he's also wearing shoes.

A shot of cold panic settles into the center of my chest. Clutching my robe at the neck, I ask, "Where are you going?"

Sean won't look at me. His movements are quick and erratic, like he wants to run from me. Sean walks across the room and closes the closet doors. He stands there for a moment, looking down at the handles before turning to me. A fake smile spreads across his lips and he heads for the door, keys in hand.

I step in front of him. "You're leaving?" I can't believe this. Sean looks at me for a full minute with pity. The floor of my stomach drops. It feels like I've been thrown off a cliff. The look he gives me says this is the way things are, but I can't accept it. My heart beats harder, as fear works its way up my spine.

"Yes." His voice is cold. "Step out of the way."

"I can't." My voice catches in my throat. The voice in the back of my mind is telling me that I'm going to regret this, that I need to step aside, but I can't. I reach for him. "Sean, stay."

A cold look crosses his face. My heart thumps in my chest like it's been shot. "I asked you to move. Don't make me force you." I don't move. I can't. I'm frozen with fear and remorse has choked me so hard that I can't speak. I don't know what expression is on my face, but it's the wrong one.

Sean grabs my arm and pulls me aside. I expect him to walk through the door without a word, but he stops. His eyes don't meet mine. There's something about him that makes me think that I'm missing something. Sean's grip loosens on my shoulder, but he doesn't let go. It feels like I'm holding him up, like he's falling apart. When he speaks, there's a hitch in his voice. "I thought I could do this, but... I can't. It's not you. I—" Dark lashes conceal his blue eyes. When Sean exhales, he looks beaten. It makes me want to fix whatever's hurting him, but I'm starting to think it's me. "I need to think."

Sean's hand slips off my shoulder and he turns away without another word. Every instinct I have says to stop him, to help him, but I know I can't. There's something there, beneath the surface and it's destroying him. It's the reason he avoids New York, it's the reason he's walking away from me. Sean disappears through the door, head hung between his shoulders.

## 32

BREATHING HARD, I watch the door slip shut. Shock washes over me. I don't know what I expected things to be like, but this isn't it. Wide-eyed, I pad over to the bed and sit down. The sheets are rumpled. The room smells like Sean and sex. I can't think. I can't breathe. The sensation worsens, growing tighter and tighter until I'm gasping for air.

Tears streak my face as I throw myself onto a

pillow. I grip it and try to suck in air, but I can't. Sean's scent hits me hard and makes me choke. I push myself up and try to get hold of my emotions. I knew this wasn't real. It's all a game. Sean is fucked up and he needs things this way. There is a reason for it. He said that over and over again, but it doesn't mesh. Nothing does. It's like there are two different versions of him. One is playful and kind. The other is so messed up that he can't fuck a girl he hasn't paid for. I clutch my face and push the tears away with the back of my hand. I've fallen for him. I can't help it.

I want to call Mel, but she's working. I need to get control over my feelings. I need to. I have to. Suddenly, the urge to go for a run hits me hard. Fresh air, the night wind in my face—all that shit will clear my head. I just need to get out of here. I glance at my ankle, wondering what Miss Black will do if I leave the building.

Screw that. I need this.

Padding to the closet, I yank the door, but it doesn't open. I pull it again, but it doesn't move. My vision is blurry from tears. I lean over and look at the handles. They lock. Sean locked the closet before he left. Rage flashes through, me so hot and hard that I can't stand it. My arm swings on its own and smashes into the door. I scream, but it doesn't make me feel better.

Wearing nothing but a robe, I turn and lean against the closet doors. I slide to the floor and hold my face in my hands. Every second I stay in this room, I feel the walls closing in around me. There's no air. I'm trapped. I tug at my hair, angry. I love him. How could I be so stupid? I close my eyes and sit there until the panic recedes. I can leave the room, but I have no clothes. I won't get very far. The hotel staff will stop me before the elevator reaches the ground floor.

My phone rings. It takes me a second to recognize the ringtone. It's Mel. I dart across the room, grabbing my purse and dumping it out on the floor. I answer just before voicemail picks up. "Mel!"

"Avery girl, are you all right? Shit, you don't sound all right. Say something. Let me hear you talk." Mel shushes someone in the background.

My voice is shaky. "I thought you were at work."

"I was. I'm done. Guy was working on speedy issues." Someone starts laughing in the background.

I recognize that chuckle. "Is that Marty?" Why are they hanging out together? They hate each other.

"Yeah, honey. Now tell me what that piece of shit did to you. Are you hurt? I'll kick his white ass myself—"

I cut her off. "No, I'm not hurt. He got mad and left. I wanted to go after him," I lie. I can't tell her that I was going to leave the building. "But he locked the closet. I can't get my clothes."

"What'd she say?" I hear Marty asking in the background.

"Shut your face, Showboat. I'll tell you later," Mel snaps at Marty. Then she says to me, "This is easy. Go look at the door." I walk over there, unsure of what she wants me to do. "What kind is it? Single door? Double doors?"

"Double. They close in the center. There's no doorjamb down the middle. The handle is the lever kind."

"Yeah, because that matters," she says sarcastically. "Haven't you ever busted into a room before?"

I stare at the phone like that's the stupidest question ever. When I put it back to my ear, I say,

"My roommate locks me out on a regular basis. What do you think?"

"Don't get fresh with me. I don't like to put my nose in other people's business. How was I...?" Marty is cracking up in the background. He's mocking her because Mel is always in everybody's business. When she speaks again, her tone is terse. She doesn't comment on Marty's giggles. "Okay, Avery, this one is easy. Look between the doors, down by the lock. If you're lucky, the lock is in there backwards and you just have to shove a credit card through the middle. If not, you have to work it in from behind."

"How do I know which way will work?" I look at it, not sure what I'm supposed to see.

"The locking part is flat. If it's in backwards, the part facing you is curved. What do you see?"

Peering through the slat in the door, I can see a gold piece of metal. "It's curved."

"Good. Pop that baby open." Mel waits while I dig through my purse and grab my debit card. I push it into the space between the two doors and it slips right in. I pull the door and it opens.

"It worked!" I say surprised. I glance at the card. Damn. That was easy.

"Of course it worked. You think I don't know stuff? Well, I do."

Marty sings in the background, "She does!"

"Shut up, Showtunes," Mel snaps at Marty. "Listen Avery, if that messed up fucker hurts you, crush the button on your bracelet."

"It's not like that," I say, as I look through the closet for my dress. Sean's coat is hanging up next to my dress. I bump the hanger and his coat falls to the floor. Something falls out of the pocket. I pick it up and look at a crumpled ball of paper. "Listen, thanks for helping. I should be home for a little bit tomorrow. I'll catch up with you guys then." I hang up the phone.

Something about the paper seems weird. Sean has this really nice coat, but has garbage in the pockets? I think it's strange, so I stick my hands into both pockets. They're empty. I didn't think he was the kind of guy to shove nasty old stuff in his coat. He's too highbrow for that.

I look at the balled up paper again and open it. In that moment, everything changes. I stare blankly at the note, not fathoming the depths of what's happening. People are like this. People do one thing and say another. It fits with Sean's words when he walked out. He thought he could do it, but he can't. Not this time. Something changed. Something's different, and now I know what it is.

I stare at the paper, reading the pretty cursive letters over and over again.

*We love you! —Amanda & Baby*

# 33

I CAN'T SWALLOW. I stare at the paper, feeling my throat grow tighter and tighter. There's a baby. He's a father. Sean is married and has a baby. Oh, holy...

I sit down hard and stare at the note. It was written hastily on a piece of computer paper. There are smudge marks, like someone grabbed it —the baby maybe. This is what he couldn't say. It had nothing to do with me. It's him. I press my eyes closed. I don't know what to do. He has a family and he's cheating—with me.

Misery bubbles up inside my chest. I wad the paper back up and put it in his pocket so it looks like I never saw it. I lock the closet door and make sure everything is back the way it was. Then, I walk into the bathroom and turn on the shower. I drop the robe to the floor and step in. I stand there, letting the water wash away every ounce of remorse I have. Sean's a dick. He's not what I thought at all. I wonder if I should confront him. It sounds insane, but I feel like I'm the one being cheated on.

He's not yours, Avery, a little voice says in the back of my mind. He never was.

This is a job. That's what it's always been to him. That's what it always will be. I swallow hard and turn off the water. After I towel off, I grab my phone and call Black.

"How are things going?" she says with her silky voice.

"Very well. I'd like to throw my name in for more work as soon as this is over." Even as I said the words, I can't believe I'm saying them. If Sean is like this, if I have to finish this job, by the time I'm done I'm going to be so emotionally repressed that it won't matter who I fuck. Maybe this is what Mel and Black meant. Maybe it's the reason why they ended up staying and taking more clients.

"Excellent, Avery." Her voice has that hollow politeness that irritates me. I hear it now, vibrating like a plucked string. "Let me make sure I understand you correctly. You don't want any time off between clients?"

"No," I say, "The sooner the better."

"I understand. Is there anything else?"

Is there? Should I tell her that I'm disillusioned? Should I tell her that I fell for Sean, but he's just a cheating jackass? I smile to myself. I sound like an idiot. "No, that's all."

I press END CALL and toss my phone back in my bag. I let the numbness overtake me. There's no other way to get through this, and I have to finish it. There's no other way to survive.

---

I LEAVE the room in nothing but my robe around 2:oo am. I'm stopped on the ground floor by the hotel manager. He's an older, squat man wearing a pristine black suit. It distracts from his round face.

"Miss Ferro," he says, taking my elbow to keep me from walking through the lobby. "May I help you with something?"

I nod. "Is Sean down here somewhere? I didn't see him at the bar."

"Yes, he is. Let me take you to him." I walk next to the man. He offers, "My name is Thomas. If you need anything, I'm happy to help. Mr. Ferro is one of our best customers and as such, we try to humor his requests. However, I would appreciate it if you wore clothes next time you came down to the lobby."

My face flames red. "Oh, I'm sorry."

"It's a perfectly honest mistake," he smiles at me, but his eyes say he knows why I'm here, what I am. We stop in front of a set of huge double doors. Thomas pulls one open and says, "Good evening, Miss Ferro."

I step through the door and stop. Blinking rapidly, I try to get my eyes to adjust to the light. I glance around at an empty ballroom. There's a grand piano in the opposite corner. Sean is sitting in front of it, playing. I don't move. For a moment, I just watch him play. Sean's eyes are closed and his dark hair hangs down over his brow. His body moves to the music like they're one and the same. The song is so somber, so dark. It tugs at my heart. I have to remind myself what Sean is, what he's done. But as I watch him play, I don't want to. I can't think about it. I don't have that luxury. I have to do this to survive. Sean's life is his to mess up. I tell myself that If Sean wants to sleep with hookers instead of his wife that it's none of my business, but I'm not that cold. I hate the idea of being the other woman, the girl that ruins a family. But that's what I am, a plaything with a high price tag.

Slowly, I pad across the room. The cold tiles chill my bare feet. Sean is still playing the lament when I come up behind him. It's a song I know well. I slip onto the bench and place my fingers on the keys. Sean glances at me, but he doesn't stop playing. I move my fingers with his, playing with him. Our shoulders brush together occasionally as I reach in front of him to press a key. Sean's blue gaze cuts to the side. He watches me as he plays. Neither of us says anything. When the song ends we both sit there, staring straight ahead.

"I'm sorry," Sean says. "I shouldn't have

walked away like that."

I find a way to act like it didn't matter. I pretend that I don't know his secret. "You don't have to explain anything to me. It's fine, Sean."

His blue eyes slip over me. Sean hesitates before saying, "You play very well. Who taught you?"

"My mother." I feel nothing. If I keep thinking it, it'll happen. Eventually I'll feel nothing. Eventually, every last part of me will go numb. I won't react to his voice or his touch. I can do this. I stare straight ahead.

"She must be a wonderful musician."

I know he's searching for kind words, but I don't care. I answer bluntly. "She was. She died along with my father in a car wreck last year. That was my favorite song. I bugged her to help me with it frequently over the past few years."

Sean watches me as I speak. Finally, he says, "You've been through a lot." It's a statement. He leaves it hanging in the air, so I nod.

"Yeah, but who hasn't?" I try to sound apathetic, but I don't pull it off. I shrug and add, "What doesn't kill you makes you stronger, or so I hear." I glance at him, expecting him to make light of it, but he just nods.

"That's what I hear, too." After a moment, he says, "What other songs do you know?"

I look at the piano in front of me. A million memories of me and my mom flash by. She loved playing classical music. I preferred darker things, more contemporary stuff. I touch the keys lightly and start playing. To my surprise, Sean joins in. Neither of us speaks. We play like that, alternating songs until sleep pulls at me so hard that I can't keep my head up.

My fingers fumble a few times and Sean stops. He turns to me and stands. Leaning over, he scoops me up and cradles me in his arms. "Avery, I'm sorry if I hurt you." He sets me down, looking into my eyes. Sean presses his lips gently to mine and a surge of guilt nearly strangles me. I do everything I can manage to kiss him back and not act like his cheating bothers me, but it does.

That night I barely sleep. I keep seeing a beautiful woman holding a sweet baby in her arms. They're just faces, something my mind dreamed up while I slept, but I feel like I stabbed them in the back. I'm not cut out for this. I wish I were dead inside. I wish I lost the ability to feel anything. I fall asleep thinking, wishing that I was someone else.

## 34

THE NEXT MORNING, Sean is gone. He slipped out without waking me. There's a note on his pillow. I open it, and think of that crumpled piece of paper in his pocket. My heart clenches. I can't breathe. Pressing my eyes closed, I chase away the pain. Inhaling slowly, I open his note.

*I'm sorry about last night. I didn't mean for things to go that way. I hope you'll take this morning off and return tonight in time for dinner. There are some more things I'll show you later. See you then.*

*-Sean*

I dress quickly and call Miss Black to tell her that Sean set me free for daylight hours. She wants me to stay put, but Sean wanted me to go out. Eventually, Miss Black folds and I leave the hotel. When I finally get back to the dorm, I can't think straight. I want to scream. I want to bury my face in my pillow and cry. The thoughts rise up and choke me so hard that I can't swallow. It's been months since I felt this crazy.

I shove the key into my door and kick it open. The door slams open wide. When I glance up, I see Amber's brain-dead boyfriend—the exhibitionist—carving a turkey on my make-up counter. Turkey juices puddle around my blushes and drip onto the floor. He smiles broadly.

"Put some pants on!" I yell at him as I run into the room.

I left the door to the hallway open. The naked jackass waves to people as they pass by. Amber isn't even here and this idiot is eating turkey on my make-up counter. I can't deal with it. I feel my heart dying inside of me. I grab a pair of sweats and change in the bathroom.

When I emerge, naked guy mutters something about joining him, but I flip him off and run out the door.

I need to get out of here. As I run down the hall, Mel sticks her head out the door. "Hey bitch! Where you running off to? I thought you were..." When I don't stop, Mel steps out into the hallway. "Avery!" She calls after me, but I don't stop. I can't stop.

It takes a minute to start my car and I'm off. I don't plan to go there. I just go wherever this crushing feeling in my chest leads me. Staring through the grime on the windshield, I drive further east. A few turns and I pull up at the black iron gates that surround the cemetery. I managed to get here without stalling. It's still early. No one is here. I drive past the rows of tombstones towards the newer plots in the back. There's an open grave, the mound of dirt is covered with green plastic grass. I drive past it and turn off the main road in the cemetery and drive to the end. I pull over. The car shudders and lurches before it stalls.

My hair hangs limp around my face. I shove open the door and walk swiftly toward them. There's a knot in my throat that I can't swallow no matter how hard I try. Tears prick my eyes, but they won't fall. My parent's plot is behind a massive oak tree. Its ancient base hides me from onlookers. I fall to my knees at the foot of my parent's grave and double over to stop the pain. My forehead rests against the cold hard ground. My teeth catch my lips and I bite and hold them between my teeth. Sucking in a rush of cold air, I sit up suddenly. My hair flies back, tossing some twigs with it. My heart hammers inside of me. It's the only thing that tells me that this hell is real. Everything else seems too wrong. I stare straight ahead, seeing their names chiseled in stone, but seeing nothing at all.

The wind lifts the ends of my hair off my shoulders. I have no idea how long I kneel here, but my legs have pins and needles. I shift my weight and sit on the ground and pull my knees into my chest. I breathe, because that's all I can do. My anger has faded over the months. I no longer come here to yell at them for abandoning me. This time I don't know why I'm here. I got in my car and this is where I ended up.

I reach for something I stashed in my pocket before running out of my dorm room. The metal feels cold against my skin. It's a little silver cross. My mother gave it to me when I turned sixteen. She said it was to remind me of what's important when things get rough. Things are worse than rough. I clutch the cross so tightly that the ends bite into my palm. Still, it doesn't stop me. Pain is something I understand. The rest of this, the senselessness of it all, eludes me.

I speak into the air. Somehow it feels normal. "What do I do, now? I didn't think my heart could break any more than it already has. The pieces still inside of me feel like broken glass. Every time I take a breath, they stab into me. It never ends..." I press my lips together and breathe.

I look down at the cross in my hand. That cross meant something to her. I wish it meant something to me, but it doesn't. All I see is a necklace. I have no faith. It died along with my parents. I string the cross around my neck and fasten the clasp. It lies against my heart. This is the closest thing I'll ever have to the comfort of hearing my Mom's voice and feeling her arms around me again. My fingers press the cross closer. I sit there, looking at nothing, barely thinking, and slowly rock myself.

Time passes. I have no idea how much, but my body has become still and cold. When a sharp breeze cuts past my cheek, I lift my face. The vacant gaze that I've had since I passed the iron gates comes into focus as I see a man in a long black coat. He stands with his shoulders hunched, looking at the roses in his hand. He stands there frozen for a long time. When he moves, he bends over and places the flowers on the ground on the grave in front of him. When he stands, he throws his head back and looks up at the sky.

I see his face. It's Sean. I don't know what I'm doing or what I want from him. I just see his pain and react. Weaving my way around countless graves, I come up behind him. My fingers clutch the cross around my neck like it can save me. My entire body has gone numb from the cold. I have no jacket. I want to feel the sting of the wind. I desperately need something to make sense.

Sean must feel my eyes on his back. He turns slowly. At first I think he's going to be mad, but his gaze sinks to the ground and he turns back to the tombstone at his feet. I walk up next to him and he asks, "What are you doing here?"

My voice comes out gravely when I speak, "Same reason as you, I suppose."

"Your parents?" he asks. His voice sounds deep and strained.

I nod, but Sean doesn't see me. I'm not sure if he sees anything. He stares straight ahead at the grave with such intensity that I can't look. "Yeah, I needed to talk to them. I have no idea if they can hear me, but I just needed to be here. I can't explain it." I'm quiet for a second and then add, "But talking to the dead seems to be a one-sided conversation. I ask them for help, but they can't help me anymore. I'm on my own."

Sean turns his grief-stricken face toward me. Our eyes lock and I see my own pain mirrored in his eyes, but there's something else there too—something more. The wind rustles his dark hair. Sean looks so lost, so vulnerable. After a moment, my eyes fall on the tombstone. I see the name. I stare at it like I don't understand. I expected this to be his parents, but it's not.

The name carved into the headstone is Amanda Ferro.

Sean turns back to the grave. I stare at the

roses he's placed on the ground. "Amanda was my wife," he says. His voice sticks to the back of his throat, barely audible. Sean doesn't say anything else.

I stare, unblinking. He was married and now Amanda is gone. The woman who wrote the note in his pocket is dead. The grave is old. There's no freshly turned soil, no indications of a recent funeral. Her death must have been years ago. Sean was much younger then, barely twenty by the look of him. I glance at the headstone again. There's only one name. Where's the baby? The lump in my throat grows as I think about what might have happened to them, about what horrors Sean had to have seen to render him the person standing next to me.

Every time I think I know what's going on, everything falls apart. I feel the anger and disappointment fracture. That wall I forced up around my heart shatters as it falls away. I reach for Sean's gloved hand and weave our fingers together. Sean lets me. We both stand there, staring, saying nothing.

Sometimes there is nothing to say.

After a few moments, he turns to me glassy-eyed. Sean's jaw is tense, like he's ready to bite someone's head off. His eyes move over my sweats and then return to my face. The wind picks up my hair and throws it over my eyes and mouth. Before I can move my hand to push it back, Sean does it for me. His eyes meet mine and he stares. I can feel him struggling to come back from the dark places in the back of his mind. I see it in his eyes and I know he can see the darkness in mine.

Part of me wants to shut down and push him out. I can't take what life is throwing at me. The sick part of the whole thing is that there's a squeaky voice in the back of my head that won't let me just lie down and die. She never gives up, even when she's had her ass handed to her time and time again.

Sean looks down at my hand and then back at my face. His voice is soft, careful. "Take me to meet them." There's a question in his words, like I have the option to say no. We watch each other carefully. Finally, I nod. I pull him onto the path and we walk back to my parent's grave in silence.

When I stop in front of them, I say, "This is Sean." I smile sadly and squeeze his hand. Sean squeezes back. We both stare at the head stone for a moment and say nothing. Finally, I say, "My mom would have liked you. She would have said you were too skinny and tried to stuff an unreasonable about of food down your throat." The thought makes me smile. She was like that, always trying to fatten up my friends.

A ghost of a smile passes over his lips. "What about your Dad?"

I smile. "Oh, he'd hate your guts. I'm sure of it."

Sean looks surprised and seriously amused. "And why is that?"

"Because you have heartbreaker written all over you. Daddy would have seen you coming from a mile away. He would have told you that he'd break every bone in your body if you hurt me." I smile thinking about it. Daddy always said it teasingly when I brought a guy home, but there was a current of truth there. He wanted to keep me safe and that meant keeping my heart in one piece. Right now my heart has broken so badly that all that is remains is dust.

The smile slips off my lips. Sean watches me. He knows what I'm thinking. It's almost like he feels the weight of the memory the same way I do. I flick my eyes to the headstone. "They got blindsided that night. So did I."

"I know what you mean." His voice is somber, deep. He adds, "What doesn't kill you makes you stronger." Sean says my words back to me, but they seem to have new meaning, like the old adage is a lie and we're the only ones who know the truth.

I nod slowly. "The thing is—I'm not stronger. I feel like I'm half dead, barely hanging on. Most days, I go through the motions, hoping the next day will be better. Then, some days bitch-slap me so hard that it feels like that night all over again." As I speak, I stare at nothing. I see nothing. The memories from that night flash through my mind. I shiver and shake it away, refusing to relive the horror again.

"And today was one of those days?" Sean says it so casually, but it's as if he knows the turmoil he caused me. I feel his eyes on the side of my face, but I don't look up. I just stare straight ahead. He sighs and looks past the tree toward his wife's grave. "Last night, something you did stirred up a memory. I couldn't repress it. That's why I left. I didn't mean to be cruel to you. I'd take it back if I could, Avery."

Sean's words should make me feel elated, but the heaviness is too great. His remorse, the pain in his voice strums through me and resonates. I know that feeling. Anything can conjure a memory—a song, a scent, a touch. I glance over at him. "I know you would."

There are more words to say, but neither of us says them. Death has fucked us both up to the point that we're barely functioning.

## 35

SEAN INSISTS on getting me coffee. As we walk back to his car, he wraps his coat over my shoulders.

"Really, I'm fine. It's better this way." I try to shirk it off and give the wool coat back to him, but Sean puts it on me again, pressing my shoulders tight.

"No, it's not. Avery, there are other things to do—ways to feel something besides pain." Sean glances at me out of the corner of his eye. When we get to his car, he pulls the door open and holds it for me.

"What makes you think that's what I'm doing?" I stop in front of him. Sean's warm breath turns white as he sighs, looking down at me.

"Can you seriously ask me that question? Now you know why I avoid New York. Now you know why I'm a deranged fuck that can't get involved with anyone, the reason why I was looking for a call girl. When Amanda died, she left a hole in my chest. Not a day goes by, that I don't feel it pulling, trying to suck me under. Some days I let it. Some days I can't stand the thought of tomorrow, of going through the motions again." Sean speaks with confidence, but his eyes say something else. His hand is clutched into a tight fist. He holds it over his heart, protecting what's left.

The pit of my stomach falls away as he speaks. I know exactly what he's talking about. "So you hired me. That's how you deal with it?" His gaze falls to the side and he nods. A year ago, I would have condemned him for saying something like that, but not now. I've been through too much to judge him. Sean's protecting himself, forcing himself to feel something besides grief. It is the same thing that I do, leaving with no coat.

"So, your sweater and lack of coat might not stem entirely from money issues, am I right?" Sean presses his forehead to mine. A light smile crosses his lips.

I look up at him from under my lashes. "No one has noticed that before. I'm not even sure I knew what I was doing. I understand feeling cold. I understand what it means and what I should do. But, my God—Sean I don't understand this." I gesture at the graveyard. "I don't know what to do. Days pass and turn into months, but nothing changes. It's not better. I feel myself getting chipped away. Soon there will be nothing left to hold on to."

My throat tightens as I speak and I drop my gaze. It feels like someone is strangling me. Admitting that I don't know how to cope with all this makes me feel weak, like I'll falter and fade away. This entire time, I've carried this massive burden on my own two shoulders. I've never said it to anyone, and here I am confessing my deepest secret to the guy who bought me.

Sean pulls me against his chest and holds on tight. I can barely feel his touch, I'm so numb. He squeezes me tighter and tighter until all the air is forced out of my lungs. That's when he loosens his grip. "There is more to hold onto than you think." He kisses my forehead and releases me.

I'm aware of the warmth, of his moist lips on my cold skin, but I can't feel the kiss. It has no comfort, no joy. It's just a touch, like pressing my finger to the tip of a needle. I've done that, just to see if I could feel the sharp pain of the needle when it pricked my skin. Instead, the only indication that I should stop was a bead of blood that dripped down my palm.

Sean's voice pulls me from the memory. "Avery, let's not waste the day just trying to muddle through it. Let's do something." Sean smiles softly at me. "We'll start with coffee and go from there." I nod.

Sean holds the door to his shiny black sports car open and I slip into the seat. When Sean gets in and turns on the car, I ask, "No motorcycle?"

"I only ride when your car is in danger of being stolen and right now," he lifts his chin toward my car, "it looks like it's in its element." His voice is lighter, his tone teasing.

"Hey!" I smile at him and add, "Don't dis my car. She's been with me through thick and thin."

"I'll have her returned to your dorm while we're out so she can continue to attract scallywags and thieves." Sean starts the car and glances over at me with a playful look on his face.

I snort laugh, not expecting his lightness. "Scallywags?"

"Yes, and that would be me. The day we met, your little car attracted both types of very virtuous men." The corner of his mouth twitches, like he wants to smile.

"Yeah, normally I'd shove everyone in the backseat and cruise up and down Deer Park Avenue blasting the radio."

That makes him smile. He pulls away from the cemetery and for the first time in a long time, I feel like I might be okay.

## 36

WITH A CUP of hot coffee in hand, Sean drives without telling me where he's going. "Seriously," I ask. "You aren't even going to give me a hint?"

Sean glances at me out of the corner of his eye. "Nope."

"Well, you suck." He chuckles, but I talk over him. "Come on, just one little hint." The hot little cup warms my hands.

"You'll have to do better than that, Miss Smith." There's a faint smile on his lips. Sean drives for a while and after a few turns, we're at a toy store.

"Reliving your childhood, are we?" I say, arching an eyebrow at him.

"Perhaps," he says, noncommittally, and walks around to open my door. I'm not used to it. I already have my hand on the door, and push it open at the same time he steps in front of the door. The result is instant. The door smacks into his waist and forces out a gush of air the same way as if a fat guy slugged his chest.

I jump out of the car. "Oh my God! I'm sorry. Are you all right?" Sean holds his hand to his stomach and bends over. He straightens but I can tell that it hurts from the way his face is pinched.

"I'm fine," he says through his teeth and tries to smile. The way he looks, something about the way he says it, makes me laugh. Placing my hand on his shoulder, I mean to offer my apologies but I can't stop laughing. My emotions are so screwed up. They turn on in short uncontrollable bursts. Suddenly, something seems very funny and I have to laugh. Maybe it's because I've cried too much over the past few months. Either way, Sean looks incredulous, which just makes me giggle more.

"Nice, very nice, Avery. I like the suave way you avoided making me feel silly." Sean laughs with me after he says it. We both lean up against the car, giggling and gasping for air.

"Thanks," I finally say, looking over my shoulder at him. "I needed that."

"I'd take a door to the gut for you any time, Miss Smith." His eyes sweep over my face. They dart between my lips and my eyes. I think he's going to kiss me, but Sean takes a deep breath and pushes off the car. The moment is gone. "Come on. Let's get what we came here for."

Sean takes me by the hand and leads me into the toy store. We have to look on the clearance aisle because the thing he wants is out of season. He's bent over, digging around in a bin when he stands and grins at me.

"Found one." Sean plucks a kite from the bin, still wrapped in plastic. It has an extra-long thing of string.

"Are you serious? We came here for a kite?" I can't imagine what he's thinking.

"Yeah. My life could use a dash of levity right now." The way he says it, the way his voice catches in his throat, makes my heart ache. I feel the same way. He can see it in my eyes. "I suspect that you are in need of the same sort of, ah... screw it." Sean runs his fingers through his hair and looks at the floor before looking back up at me. "I'm trying to sound classy, Avery, but your eyes just make me melt. I can't think around you. You bring out a side of me that, well, let's just say that it hasn't seen sunlight in years. Let's go fly a kite at the beach. I'll buy you lunch. We can see how high the thing goes before the string snaps and it flies away. What do you say?"

Stepping toward him, I touch the plastic packaging on the little kite. It's the ninety-nine cent kind that kids fly. The corner of my lips pull up. "Well, I have plans this evening, but I think I can sneak in a trip to the beach to fly this..." Turning the package over, I look to see what cartoon character is on the kite. But when I flip it over, I laugh so hard that I slap my hands over my mouth. Giggling, I point to the kite. "Holy shit. That's a pig in a tutu! On a kite!"

Sean grins, "When pigs fly. Apparently, a

very pretty pig will be flying today." He holds out his elbow. "My lady."

Laughing, I take his arm and embark on one of the best days of my life.

## 37

I KICK off my shoes as Sean pulls the little kite out of the package and assembles it. The beach is empty today, probably because it's freezing. The sun is a bright golden ball and the sky is an awesome shade of blue. I sit down and bury my toes in the sand, not caring about the chilly air.

Sean drops his coat on the sand next to me and ties the string onto the kite. "Here you go. Ladies first." Sean hands me the kite and I take it.

I can't help but smile when I look at the thing. It has a pink cartoon pig doing a pirouette in a purple tutu. It's perfect.

"Just so you know, I suck at kite flying. Kites hate me. You've been warned." I nod at him, but Sean gives me a quizzical look.

"How could you possibly suck at kite flying?"

"Wait and see. It's the kind of suckage that's spectacular."

"Oh," he grins, saying, "the best kind of suckage, then." Sean takes the kite from my hands and walks a few steps back, after kicking off his shoes. The wind blows his dark hair out of his eyes. For the first time I get to see his face without that brooding look he always wears. Sean has a boyish grin on his face as he moves away from me holding the silliest kite that I've ever seen. "Ready?" he asks, and holds the kite over his head.

I nod. "Yup."

Sean releases the kite and I turn and run forward. The wind catches the kite quickly, pulling it higher and higher. I yank the line and let out more string and stop running. Then, I yank it again as the piggy kite swerves in the air. The wind pulls it hard and the kite changes direction. Sean is still standing in the same spot, looking up at the kite when it happens. I have no idea why it happens to me, but it does. The kite seems to get caught in a little vortex, swirls, and plummets—and I mean drops like a speeding vulture—from the sky. Sean's eyes grow wide. He runs at the last second and the kite crashes into his hip. He yelps and rubs his thigh.

I try not to laugh, but I can't hide the smile on my face. "I told you that I'm cursed. I can't fly a kite worth a damn. It doesn't matter where you stand. It will hit you." The wind catches my hair and tosses it behind me.

"I don't believe it," Sean says shaking his head as he walks toward me. "There is no way in hell you could hit me like that twice." Sean is standing next to me, winding up the string. He hands me the roll back and takes the kite. "Ready?"

"Hell, yeah. I'm fine. The kite isn't going to hit me. Maybe you should put on your helmet?" I tease him, grinning. I know how this is going to go. Sean's blue eyes lock with mine. A shiver runs through me and it has nothing to do with the crisp air.

"If you hit me again, I'll wear my helmet."

"Is that a challenge, Mr. Jones?"

"Are you doing it on purpose, Miss Smith? Were you a professional kite flyer or something?"

I laugh and shake my head. "No, it's just my natural awesomeness manifesting itself." I smile at him for a moment. "You know it's going to crash into you, right? I mean, this seems like we're tempting fate way too much."

"Fly the kite, Smitty." Sean steps away from me, spooling the string out as he walks. When he's a few feet away, Sean asks me if I'm ready.

I nod and he releases the kite. I tug the string hard and run a few steps. Sean moves this time and walks toward me. He watches the kite climb higher and higher.

I yank the string and the give it more slack. The piggy kite flies higher. Sean has that arrogant grin on his face, like he thinks he's won. He stands in the sand next to me and folds his arms over his chest. He's wearing jeans with a charcoal colored sweater. That color makes his eyes look like topaz.

Sean makes a pleased noise in the back of his throat. "The kite's still in the air."

"I didn't say that I couldn't keep it up," I grin at him. "That would be a totally different problem. I said that it will crash into you. To crash, the kite needs to come down. And it will hit you."

"That was a fluke. You can't honestly tell me that you've flown a kite in the past few years and it crashed into someone every time?"

"I could say no, but it'd be a big fat lie. Have a seat Mr. Jones and wait for it to happen." I tug the kite string and watch the piggy in the tutu dance against the sky.

Sean settles onto the sand next to me. He pulls up his knees and wraps his arms around them. "I used to come here a lot. It didn't matter what the weather was like."

I nod and glance at him out of the corner of my eye. "The best time to be here is—"

"Right before a storm," we say in unison.

Sean gives me a strange look, which I return. Smirking I tug on my piggy kite. A prickly feeling covers my skin and is gone in a flash. I tuck my hair behind my ear, but the wind keeps whipping it in my face. "Well, that was creepy. Most people say in the sunshine."

"You aren't most people."

"Neither are you," I say. My heart is pounding. I don't turn to look at him. I can feel his gaze resting on the side of my face. I tug the kite. "I like how the air feels thick and the waves crash onto the sand. I like to put my toes in the sand when it has that damp chill. I've come out in the rain, and just sat on the shore. There's something about the ocean, about the waves and watching a spring storm roll in that's soothing."

Sean stares at me. When he doesn't respond, I look over at him. His blue eyes are wide. When our gazes meet, they lock. I can't look away. Something inside me responds to him, to the way he looks at me. I feel the tug at the core of my body telling me that he's more than he seems. I try to force the sensation back, but I can't.

For a moment, Sean just breathes. When his lips part to say something, I feel the kite string go slack. Before the words are out of his mouth, the kite collides with his head. It falls to the sand in a pile of plastic and string. Sean jumps a mile, and holds his hand to his ear.

I step toward him, my feet getting tangled in string. "Are you all right?" I kneel in front of him and turn his face to the side.

Sean's hands fall away from the spot where he was hit. There's a little scrape on his cheek that's beading with blood. I reach into my pocket and take out a tissue. I press it to his skin and hold it there. I feel stupid for hurting him. Sean takes my hand in his. When I feel his gaze, I turn and look into his eyes. The wind ruffles his hair, tossing it every which way. He looks at me like he's never seen me before. The expression worries me. My stomach flips in response.

I manage, "I'm sorry."

Sean doesn't answer. He just watches me, intently focused on my face. Sean's eyes drift to my mouth. After a moment, he leans in and kisses me lightly. My lashes lower as he does it and my heart pounds harder. Sean pulls back slightly, and looks into my eyes. He opens his mouth like he's going to say something, but nothing comes out.

My voice is so sweet, so soft. I cup his face between my hands and say, "Oh, no. Did that blow to the head break your brain?"

Sean seems to come back from wherever his mind drifted off to. The panic in his eyes vanishes. I have back the flirt with the bike, the man with the kite. "If I'm bludgeoned by a piggy kite and lose my mind, you have to promise to tell people that I was done in by something much more manly."

I nod slowly, smiling. "Mmm. Bear attack. There are bears all over the beach. Totally believable." I wink at him.

"That mouth is going to get you in trouble," Sean says, smiling. The look in his eye is playful and carefree.

The kite is behind him. I lean forward, like I'm going to hug him. Sean tenses slightly. I have no idea why. We've had sex, how is he still tense when I touch him? The hug was a diversion anyway. I reach behind him and grab the kite.

Smacking the kite into his back, I giggle, saying, "Bear attack! Bear attack! Roar!"

Sean's jaw drops open. He lets me smack him with the kite at least three times before he tackles me, and knocks me back into the sand. Sean's fingers find my bare skin under my sweater and he tickles. I laugh and continue to taunt him. "Next time we should get a bear kite. That way it's more believable. Millionaire, Sean Ferro, attacked on Jones Beach, by a bear. Channel 12 will come running out if we call that in." I reach into my pocket, or rather I try to, but Sean yanks the phone away.

"I'm not a millionaire and Channel 12 doesn't cover bear attacks—too exciting." He pins me down, and manages to straddle me. Sean's breathing hard. He looks down at my face and I go still.

"You're not rich?"

"I didn't say that. I said I'm not a millionaire." Sean has a strange look on his face.

"Ah, since we're playing coy, I'm not a millionaire, either. I'm a twentyaire. I have twenty-five bucks in my pocket until I get paid." I try to pull my wrists free, but Sean doesn't budge. "So, come on. What are you? I told you how much I'm worth." I smile at him, laughing. "By the way, I'm paying for lunch. The $1 menu at Wendy's has some bitchin' chicken nuggets with your name on them." I waggle my eyebrows at him, not expecting him to tell me anything.

"You're treating me?" he asks, surprised. I nod. Sean pauses for a second. Then he licks his lips and leans down and whispers in my ear. "I'm a billionaire, maybe a few times over."

I giggle when he pulls back and say, "Like the Monopoly man?" I stare at him. Holy shit. Sean watches me, waiting to see how I take it. I act like I'm going to be serious, and ask, "Do you have that kickass top hat? Nah, I bet you're more of a monocle man." I reach into his pocket and Sean squirms.

He grabs my wrists and pins me again. "Seriously? That's your reaction? You ask me if I dress like a cartoon character?" My eyes shift back and forth between his. Sean seems surprised.

I'm more distracted by his eyes. I shrug. "Money's money. You need it to live, but beyond that, I don't care. You can't take it with you. Hey, and this doesn't mean that I'm going to stiff you on lunch. Don't worry. I'll get you a drink and some fries, too. What's mine is yours." I grin at him, expecting him to laugh, but he doesn't. The pressure on my wrists disappears as Sean sits up. He slips off of me and I sit up next to him. "Did I say something wrong?" I ask, tucking my hair behind my ear. "Because I do that a lot. I didn't mean to be ass-y Avery."

Sean glances at me. "You seriously only have twenty bucks?" I nod. "And you were going to spend most of it on me, today?"

I nod again. The way he's acting makes me nervous. I try to play it off, like it's nothing. "It's not rocket science, Sean. We're hungry. We eat."

Sean's eyes scan my face, like he can't believe

what he sees. "You really don't have any desire to be rich?"

"There's a line between being piss-ass poor and having enough to get by. I want to hit the get-by line, maybe a little bit more." I shrug and pull my knees into my chest. "More than that just fucks things up. Life isn't about money. It's about the people you love—the relationships you make. Maybe I have that once poor always poor thing. I don't know, but I don't really care, Mr. Jones. If you have a problem with it—"

Sean stares at me like I have two heads. "I don't have a problem with it, not at all."

I wiggle my toes in the sand and say, "Can't buy me love."

To my surprise, Sean says the next line of the song. I smile at him. Sean continues to recite the verse and soon his words turn to song. The velvety sound of his voice sounds perfect. Sean pulls me to his chest and sings just for me. I relax, looking out at the ocean and watch the waves. His fingers smooth my hair as his breath warms my cheek. It makes that feeling in my chest stir, the good one. For the longest time, the only thing I could feel was that hollow ache.

38

SEAN NUZZLES his chin to the side of my face and holds me tight. I'm sitting between his legs on the sand. The way he breathes makes me feel peaceful. It's strange. I don't understand why or how. I don't question things like that anymore. I just take it for what it is—I feel at ease around him. Sean rubs his hands over my arms. The chill in the air numbed my skin a while ago. It feels good to have him sitting so close, to warm me up.

I tilt my head back to ask him something, but never get the chance. When our eyes meet, something shifts. All day Sean has acted more like a friend than a lover. I've convinced myself it's because that's what he is. I'm his paid lover. It's not the same. But that look in his eye ensnares me. It pulls me to him, making the butterflies in my stomach flutter to life.

Sean watches my lips with a hungry intensity that sends sparks through my body. Through lowered lashes, his eyes never stray from my mouth. I'm pulled to him. With everything in me, I try to resist, but I can't. I'm barely breathing, hardly holding on. Sean gives me something to hold on to, at least for now.

The space between us closes. Sean's lips are right there. I feel the magnetic pull and before I know it, his lips are brushing against mine. I suck in air, trying hard to control myself. I don't want him to know how enamored I am, how much I want him. It has nothing to do with contracts or money. It's Sean. I want him, I want to be around him and taste his lips because I want to.

The kiss is a breathtaking tease. When he pulls away, Sean's blue eyes are blazing like twin flames. I can't look away. I twist in his lap and turn to my side. Leaning into his chest, I lift my hand to his cheek. Leaning in slowly, watching his beautiful lips, I close the space between us. My heart pounds harder as I feel Sean's hands in my hair. He doesn't pull me forward, but he doesn't push me back.

Something inside of me is screaming for me to stop. It's the voice that tells me to hold on, that I can survive this. When every other thought falls silent, it's always there. I don't understand the warning bells going off. I just know how Sean makes me feel and I need to feel something that I understand right now. That night on the motorcycle, the night he helped me chase my car down, there were no voices telling me to beware. He could have ridden off with me and dumped my body at the Captree boat docks. No one would have known what happened to me. There was no little voice in the back of my head then, so it's totally weird that it's there now.

Breathing in deeply, I ignore the warning and press my lips to his. The uncertainty fades as Sean kisses me back. His tongue sweeps against the seam of my lips, gently, asking me if I want him. When I let him in, Sean holds me tight and leans us back into the sand. He rolls so that I'm under him. The cold air and the hot kisses crash together. My pulse pounds harder as the kiss builds hotter and hotter. Sean keeps his lips on mine the entire time, not stopping for breath. His hands touch my face, gently stroking my cheek as the kiss intensifies. My heart thuds inside of me like it's been sleeping and suddenly startled awake. My body is hot and cold, my mind is swimming in sensations that conflict.

Sean knows how to draw me out of my despair. His touch is like magic. Everything that was crushing me is gone, temporarily held away. I lose myself in his lips. My eyes are closed and I focus on the feel of his lips on mine. Every time he sweeps his tongue over mine, my insides flutter. It's magic.

After a moment, Sean pulls back. His eyes sweep my face before locking with mine. Reaching toward me, Sean tucks a dark curl behind my ear. "Your kiss is addicting," he says, his voice a little too husky from a kiss. I smile at him and touch his cheek and feel the light stubble under the pads of my fingers. Sean's eyes lower as I do it. He takes a slow, deep, breath like he's savoring my touch. When his eyes open again, he takes a jagged breath. My gaze drifts to his lips. I can't stop staring at his mouth. "If you keep looking at me like that, I'm not going to be able to stop."

An awkward smile spreads across my face. My fingers twirl the hair at the base of his neck. "You'd have sex in the sand, when it's freezing outside?"

"If it meant that I could be with you," his hand strokes my cheek, "then, yes."

I stare into Sean's eyes, unable to blink, unable to breathe. This feels real. I don't know what to say. "You get to be with me as much as you want. You bought me, remember?"

Sean's eyes dart back and forth between mine. His hand strokes my cheek again. The sensation makes my eyes close briefly as his warm fingers trail across my chilled skin. "But it's not like this."

Before I can ask him what he means, Sean's lips are on mine. He kisses me fiercely, pressing his mouth firmly to mine. His hands rove my body, carefully moving over areas that no one is supposed to touch. His hands slip over the curve of my hips and under my sweater. I feel Sean's cold fingers press against the small of my back. I arch toward him and Sean pulls me tighter. He kisses me like he's never going to get another chance.

My fingers tangle in his hair. I find the bottom of his sweater and slip my hands underneath. I slide my palms along his toned body, feeling the warm skin on his back. Sean reacts by moving onto me. My knees part and I wrap my ankles around his. The kisses grow more passionate. My heart pounds harder. I don't understand how he does this to me. In that moment, there's only him and me. I don't hurt. There are no memories to repress, no thoughts to hold back. There's only Sean and his hot lips.

Without realizing it, I pull his hair. Sean gasps and breaks the kiss. His eyes are dark with desire. He's breathing hard and so am I. Watching me closely, Sean reaches for the button on my jeans. He flips the button with his thumb and lowers the zipper. My pulse is thundering in my ears, waiting to see what Sean wants to do. His blue eyes are locked on mine. Sean presses his hand to my stomach and slips his fingers into my panties. My mouth falls open into a little O. I make a sound at the back of my throat as his fingers touch me. Sean watches me and gages my reactions to his touch. He moves his hand in a way that makes me hot even though it's cold.

Sean's fingers tease me, pressing and flicking the sensitive flesh. I gasp and push my hips to his hand, wanting more. He watches me move. Our eyes lock. There's something about his gaze that captivates me. I never thought I'd want someone to do this to me, and watch me so openly, but with him it feels right. When I can't stand the teasing anymore, I wrap my fingers around Sean's neck and pull him back down. Kissing Sean fiercely, I feel his hand shift lower. His fingers push inside of me. Gasping, I rock my hips against his hand. Sean dips his fingers in and out, rocking with me. The movement makes me feel like I'm floating. I never want it to end. I feel his eyes on me, watching me. My heart pounds harder. I feel what he's done to me, how my body responds to him. The heat between my legs warms my entire body.

Sean's lips press against my cheek and then dip to my neck. I hear voices coming from somewhere behind us on the boardwalk. Sean hears them, too. He stills for a moment and the people walk past. Sean is breathing hard when he looks at me.

"Tell me what you want," Sean says, his voice filled with need.

"You." It's the only thing I want. I want to feel Sean inside of me. I want to lose myself in him.

I reach for his jeans and undo the button. When my hands are on the zipper, he stops me. Sean's fingers hold mine. There's a slight tremor to his hands. When I look at his face, Sean won't return my gaze. I can barely breathe. Sean seems like he's frozen. I must have done something, but I don't know what. Taking his hand, I lift it to my lips. I kiss each one of his fingers, gently pressing my lips to the soft pad. Then, I take the next finger and do it again. When I finish, I reach for his waist again.

This time, Sean lets me. I lower his zipper and slip my hand below his jeans. Sean sucks in the cold air as my fingers wrap around his hard, hot shaft. I free him from his cloths without undressing him, and then pull him onto me. Sean adjusts my jeans, lowering them. When the cold air hits my warm bottom, I think I might die. But then Sean is there, hot and hard.

I feel his body against mine. Sean pushes into me slowly and then pulls nearly all the way out.

Then he repeats it. My hands find the skin on his back. Every time he pushes into me, I dig my nails in wanting more. Every moment that passes is filled with pure bliss. My body responds to him, but it's so different than the other night. I feel different. My core is hotter than hell and that delicate throbbing starts somewhere inside of me. Sean thrusts into me in rhythm with that pulsing. As he takes me higher and higher, the throbbing becomes more demanding. When he can't take it anymore, Sean thrusts into me, pushing harder and faster, until I shatter. Gasping, every inch of my body feels incredible. I'm so high, so intoxicated with him.

Sean stays there, on top of me, breathing hard. His fingers brush my hair out of my face. The look on his face is pensive. Sean's gaze sweeps over my eyes, cheeks, and lips. His mouth parts like he wants to say something, but he doesn't. A shiver slips down my spine. Suddenly I feel the cold sand and damp air. I'm still warm, but my senses are returning. I'm falling back to earth, becoming more aware of what we did.

Sean rolls off of me and helps me get my jeans up without filling them with sand. As it is, there's sand stuck to my cheeks and the small of my back. We wiggled too much to be sand-free. After he buttons my jeans, Sean lays back down, pressing his body to mine. That distant look in his eyes is gone, replaced with something that I don't recognize. There's a softness there, a vulnerability that makes me want to hold him forever. Sean presses his lips together. I think he's going to say something, but he can't seem to say it. I start to speak, but Sean leans down and presses his lips to mine, silencing me. The kiss is small and chaste. His mouth drifts to my cheek, and then my eyes and nose, leaving a trail of light kisses in his wake. The last kiss is on my forehead.

I watch him, wondering what he's thinking, wishing that I knew. I finally ask, "What are you thinking?"

Sean sits up on the sand and lets out a rush of air. He pushes his hands through his hair and looks down at me. "I wish things were different. I wish I..." He sounds tense, like he made a mistake. The muscle in his jaw tightens like he can't swallow.

I sit up and lean back on my elbows. The wind catches my hair and lifts it from my neck, chilling me. I jump up. I reach out and take

Sean's hand and pull him to his feet. "This isn't the time for wishing or regrets."

Sean looks at my hands holding onto his. When his gaze lifts, he asks, "Then what time is it?" There's more there, things he wants to say. I can hear his heart breaking all over again. I wonder if I'm echoing his wife. I wonder if he feels guilty. I know loss, but Sean's is different. I can't imagine his pain.

"Time for lunch. I'm treating. You're driving. Come on, motorcycle man. Carpe diem and all that crap. Let's go!" I bend over and grab the piggy kite and we head for the car.

Neither of us says anything for a while. Sean seems lost, like he's floating with no anchor. I lean back in the seat, grateful for the heater. Maybe I'm a little nuts, always making myself cold, but that doesn't mean that I don't like getting warm. I like things that are predictable, things that I can control. It makes me feel better.

We head into Wendy's and I tell Sean to grab us a table. He lifts an eyebrow at me. "You're ordering for me? That's kind of manly."

"Get over it, bitch," I tease, smiling at him. I meant it to sound more serious, but he smiles and I laugh. "Go sit. Let me treat you to the most wonderful lunch of your life." I lean in and whisper in his ear, "It's that good."

Sean walks away and I order us a bunch of stuff off the cheap-o menu. This is a splurge for me, but it's worth it. I get the idea that Sean doesn't dine on a $1.99 very often. I wonder what expression he'd have on his face if saw my dorm room and my stash of Ramen noodles. The naked guy would probably be a distraction. Where the hell did he get a turkey from, anyway? I wonder if Amber's plaything stole it from the cafeteria.

I smile to myself and walk back to the table. Sean looks at the tray and back up at me. "Milkshakes?"

"Don't come between a girl and her chocolate. Here," I hand him a small burger, half the fries, and a cup of chili. Taking the burger, I unwrap it and pull the bun off. I spoon the chili onto the meat, followed by the fries, and then a dollop of the shake. "Happy lunch."

Sean looks at the sandwich like it might bite him. He tilts his head sideways and looks at the frozen shake melting out the side of the sandwich. "And you can assure me that I won't die from eating this?" He lifts it and takes a bite.

There's a crazy-ass expression on his face, like he can't decide if it's delicious or disgusting.

I shrug my shoulders as I make my own weird little burger. "I don't know. This is the first time I've put these together." When I put the bun back on and lift the burger to my mouth, Sean's blue eyes are wide. He's staring at me. "What?"

"I'm waiting to see if you're screwing with me or if you plan on eating it, too." He's smiling, like he's trying not to laugh.

"Oh, I'm eating it." I grin at him and stuff the food in my mouth, taking a huge bite. The lettuce and ice cream are cold, while the rest of it is hot. The textures and tastes mix in mouth.

Sean watches me chew. "What's your verdict?"

I smile and wipe some chocolate from the corner of my mouth. "It's the most confusing thing I've ever eaten. It's sweet and salty, hot and cold. It's like the bipolar burger."

"Created by the slightly insane spray-start car girl," Sean says smiling at me. He takes another bite and makes a strange face when he swallows. I can't believe he's eating it. "I still can't decide if it's good or gross."

I point a fry at him and say, "Eat the whole

thing and then decide."

"I think you're just trying to see what you can put in my mouth, Miss Smith." Sean's eyes sparkle as he leans across the table and speaks in that velvety voice of his.

I poke him in the nose with a french fry. "I already know what I can put in your dirty mouth, Mr. Jones."

He feigns shock and presses his fingers to his chest. "And I've barely told you about myself. My, my, what keen eyes you have...amongst other things." There's an older guy at the next table. He glances at Sean, his eyes wide.

My face flames red. I hide behind my burger, acting like I'm going to take a bite, but it just hovers in front of my face. Sean presses a finger to the food and pushes it back to the table. I glance up at Sean. There's a wicked look in his eye. "How can you be so shy after what we just did? There were people, Avery, and you didn't even pause. But this, talking about it later, this makes you blush?" He's laughing, smiling at me, teasing.

I slap his arm. "I'm a complicated person, what can I say?"

The man next to us clears his throat. He's

thin, with leathery looking skin and silver hair. A green ball cap sits on his head. He's wearing a flannel jacket. With his tray in his hand, he stands and says to me, "Be careful with that one." His eyes flick to Sean as he passes us, like the old guy doesn't like him.

The smile fades off of Sean's lips, but I call after the guy. "Actually it's the other way around."

The old guy gives me a look when he dumps the trash off his tray. He walks out without another word.

"So, random men warn you away from me and that's your response?" Sean looks at me oddly. I can't tell if he's playing with me or really wants to know.

"Random men say lots of things to me. One guy was like, that guy stole your car! He was really sexy. Turns out that he's a bit of a sex fiend." I laugh lightly and smile at him. Sean's eyes hold mine and I feel my stomach sink. I said the wrong thing.

But Sean glazes over it. "I was kind of shocked. Most girls would scream and call the cops if they got carjacked."

I point a fry at him and say, "I'm not most

girls. I flashed half of Long Island that night jumping on and off your bike."

Sean watches me. I can tell he's going to say something terrible. I don't want to hear it. I try to talk over him, but he puts his hand over mine and cuts me off. "You know that things can't stay like this, don't you? I'm not this guy."

I don't understand what he means. How can he not be himself? But, suddenly his words snap into place. There's a darker version of Sean. This lighter one isn't real. It's an illusion. I pull my hand away and pick at my food. "That's fine. I'm not this girl."

"Avery," he snaps, with a "be serious" tone.

"Sean," I mimic him back, using the same voice. "Don't tell me what I do or don't see. I know you're a fucked up mess, okay. So am I. I'm okay with it."

"You don't know what you're talking about." His voice is cold, warning. The rest of the meal passes in tense silence. I don't know what to say to him. After everything that happened today, I feel closer to him and this feels like he's pushing me away. I don't understand why. Every time things seem okay, he acts like this. It's driving me crazy.

Sean's gaze doesn't meet mine while he finishes eating. It's like he's stuck somewhere in the back of his mind. I wonder if he can't come out of that darkness or if he doesn't want to. The entire time I'm with him, I notice something. We're very alike in how we dealt with the lot we were given, but there's a cynical sharpness to Sean that I don't have. He seems to guard it, carefully wielding it when someone gets too close. That smile on his face, the one he wore that night at the steakhouse, is fake. His entire façade is a house of cards. I can't blame him for doing anything he needs to do to hold himself together. I don't pretend to know how he feels about his loss. It's almost like he blames himself, that it was more than misfortune that stole his wife. I glance at his beautiful face and wonder about his child. I can't imagine Sean giving the baby away, not if that child is the last piece he has of his wife. But Sean doesn't mention the baby.

My throat tightens thinking about it. Sean's lived through hell and hides every last bit of it. Watching him at the cemetery was the first glimpse I got of who he really is, and every time that I think I know Sean, I find out that I don't know him at all.

After lunch, Sean drives me back to campus. The silence continues, until he turns onto the main road. "Do I need to pretend that I don't know where you live? Or would you like me to drop you by your dorm?"

I glance at him. How does he know which dorm I'm in? I wonder if I should be concerned, but I'm not. Not looking at him, I say, "Wherever is fine." My emotions feel brittle like an old leaf. I'm afraid I'm going to lose myself and never crawl out of the grief that's drowning me.

Sean pulls up in front of my dorm. I get out and see my car parked at the end of the lot. Before I shut the door, I turn back. "Thank you." My voice is wrong. It sounds like I'm saying something else, something I should never say to him. I love you. I hold his gaze for a moment and try to swallow, but I can't.

Sean nods. "Thank you. I'll remember today for a very long time."

My throat tightens. Why does it feel like we're saying good-bye? I push back the feelings, and nod at him. I close the door and walk away, thinking I'll see him in a few hours. But, I'm wrong.

# 39

AS I WALK toward my room, I pass Mel, who darts from her room when she sees me walk by. I don't feel like talking and I need to change.

Mel doesn't seem to care though, and yanks me by the elbow. "Whoa! Where do you think you're going?" I whirl around and catch my balance before I fall over. Sand falls out of my pant leg onto the dingy gray carpet. Mel glances at the sand and back up at me. She crosses her arms over her ample chest and throws out her hip. Her head sways as she scolds me. "Have you lost your mind? I saw you with that guy on the beach. You can't date anyone. Get your ass in here." When I don't move and flick my eyes longingly down the hallway, she snaps her fingers. "Now."

I sigh. "Fine. Whatever." I follow her into her room. Her roommate is out. Mel has at least nine books open with pages marked with little sticky notes. She's working on her research project.

"Don't give me that shit, Avery. I saw you and if I saw you, Black could have." She shuts the door. After moving a book, she extends her hand to the chair I usually take when I visit her room. "Sit, and tell me what the hell you're thinking. Black won't pay you a cent if you violate your contract, which—by the way—you did by making out with some guy on the beach."

My eyes feel tired, strained. I glance up at her. "How'd you find me?"

She cocks her head to the side and makes a face. "Do you think I'm stupid?" Tapping her finger to her lips, she says, "Let's see, what are the three places Avery runs off to when she's psychotically upset?" Mel ticks them off on her finger as she lists my three places. "One, that shitty old church out in timbuk-fucking-tu, which is a hell of a drive to make when you're not already out there. Two, your parent's grave. And three, Jones Beach, Field five. Seriously, what the hell is going through your head?" She folds her arms over her chest and taps her foot. Mel is still standing in front of me. I know she's scolding me because she knows what's at stake—everything, my whole life.

I don't look at her when I speak. "I didn't realize you knew all those places."

"A girl can't have a brain? Since your parents died, I know exactly where to find you when you go into that super funk, but Avery—after everything you went through to get that job and you already did the nasty with a client—why are you throwing it away?" Her arms fall to her sides and her voice softens a little.

"I'm not," I say, feeling emotionally barren. "The guy on the beach was Sean. I ran out to the cemetery. You're right about that." She nods like damn straight I'm right. I glance up at her. "Please sit. Today's been hard and I really don't need you towering over me like you're going to strangle me."

Mel grumbles and then plops down on her bed. "Go on."

"Sean was there. I didn't see him at first." I feel the story stick in my throat. I don't want to talk about it, but I need to. I tell her about the paper that fell out of his coat, his wife's name, about what I thought. "But I was wrong. She died and I don't know what happened to the baby, he doesn't talk about it. He's hollow, like me." I'm staring into nothing as I speak. My voice echoes in my ears. I feel like I'm not even here anymore.

"Bullshit." Mel rushes toward me, which shocks the hell out of me. Grabbing me by the shoulders, she pins me back in the chair. She shakes me hard, yelling in my face as she does it. "Wake the fuck up!" Mel releases me. I blink rapidly and look at her like she's nuts. "You think this is a game? You don't have the luxury to have that spaced out look on your face. One mistake Avery, just one goddamned mistake will send you into cardboard-box-land and you'll never come back.

"This was a mistake. You're falling for him. That's a bigger mistake. There's nothing there for you. The guy is fucked up beyond repair. He hired a call girl so he wouldn't have to deal with whatever shit happened to him. It's none of your business. He's not yours. He never will be, so stop thinking about him like that.

"This will ruin you, Avery. Maybe you don't see it yet, but I sure as hell do. And you're not like him. I know you think you are, I see it on your pasty face, but you're not. He has no soul. That guy is dead inside. You aren't. You're still fighting. Don't give up, girl. As your best friend, as a girl who's had her share of shit, don't surrender. You and me, we're survivors. You're going to get through this. You're going to finish college, get your master's degree, and get the hell out of here. I know you will."

Mel's passion is contagious. I feel incredibly stupid for moping around, for attaching myself to someone who doesn't want me. Swallowing hard, I ask, "How do you know? I mean, Sean seems—"

Mel leans toward me and places her hand on my shoulder. "Listen. I'm going to tell you how I know, and don't think that I'm mean. I'm just telling you what's real, okay?" I nod slowly. Fear pulses through my body. I can already tell that I'm not going to like what she has to say. "That guy doesn't love you. He's not even into you. He came to Black and asked for a virgin. That was it,

Avery. You were the only one, so he took you. I was there when he called. He wanted a curvy blonde. Black said all we had was you. You're not his type. You're a warm pussy to fuck and nothing more. Avery, do your job and get the hell away from him." She tightens her grip on my shoulder.

I can't look at her. Inside my head, I know that's all I am. I'm a hooker, but sometimes it feels like more. My jaw locks as she speaks. When I try to talk, I work it to loosen the tense muscles. "You're right. I know you're right..."

"And?"

"And, nothing. I'm nothing to him. All this is new to me. I can't separate my heart from my body." I blink slowly, trying to get the burning sensation in my eyes to stop.

Mel sits down across from me, but still within reach. "Admitting that it's just sex is the first part. Doing it over and over again is what steels your heart. When you do it that way, you don't know who they are and you won't care. It's money, it's a stress-reliever, it's fun—but it's never love. Avery, you've got to remember that. They want no strings, no emotional attachment, and that's what we give them." Mel pauses for a second and then glances at me, like she shouldn't be asking. "What do you think about taking another client? It would help you get over this one."

"I already told Black that I would." My chest feels like it's going to cave in. The pressure is too much.

"Good. Good." Mel pats my knee. "That's the first step out of this. When you do it with another guy, you'll see that what you feel for Sean is just a trick your mind's playing on you; that it was only fucking. If you told Black that you want another client, she'll have you agree to the person and sign the contract tonight before going to Sean. Sign them. Don't wait. It'll keep things from getting more muddled. You can do this, Avery. It's a good job." Her eyes are so vibrant. She's leaning toward me, trying to hold my gaze.

I nod slowly, like I'm stuck in a vat of gelatin. "I know it is, but I don't know if I can shut him out. How do I do that?" I ask, glancing up at her. I feel so lost, so alone. I bury my face in my hands and breathe.

"It's a job, Avery. Keep things that way. Let him lead and don't kiss him, don't give the chance for anything else. The guy has got to have some fetish shit going on. Drag it out of him and do it. That'll shatter your prince charming version of him real fast." She pats my knee again, and then grabs my hands and pulls me up. "You need some fun." I start to protest, but she waves me off. "No, I know you gotta get ready, but you'll like this fun. Come on."

Mel drags me down the hallway and stops in front of my door. She grins at me with mischief her eyes. Mel presses her fingers to her lips, telling me to be quiet. Then she turns the knob and kicks open the door. The door makes a loud thud. Naked guy is standing at the counter. He jumps a mile. I can't believe he's still here. I look around for Amber. The light in the bathroom is on and the shower is running.

Mel walks in, sashaying her hips and making a beeline for naked dude. I follow her in and watch, leaving the door open behind me.

"Hey, ladies," he grins at us, "Is it time for a threesome? I got my—" The smile falls off his face. Concern flashes in his eyes when he sees Mel coming for him.

"I want you to take your skinny ass out of this room and never come back." As she walks, Mel passes the turkey carcass and takes the carving knife. Mel flips it in her hand like she's a ninja. My mouth falls open. So does naked guy's.

He lifts his palms, "Ladies, please. I can do you both separately. That's not a problem." His normal bravado is gone. His voice sounds like it's stuck in his throat. Mel flips the knife. It turns handle over blade several times and then she catches it in her hand.

"Sure, Pasty. Let's do it. I've got a bit of a pain fetish though, so let's just say that this won't be pleasant—for you." Mel smiles at him.

Naked guy doesn't speak. He glances across the room. His clothes are at the foot of Amber's bed. He smiles at Mel like he's going to say yes, then turns on his heel and runs. Naked guy nearly knocks me over, muttering crazy bitches under his breath and tears down the hallway. Laughter follows in his wake. Mel grins at me, and stabs the knife into the cutting board.

A few seconds later, we see naked guy running across the quad, out the window. I laugh. Apparently his exhibitionism was only for a lucky few ladies, because he's screaming like a lunatic as he runs for the bookstore. I wonder if he plans on buying new clothes or hiding in the stacks.

"You knife juggling nut," I say to Mel, laughing.

"Nobody plays wussy games like darts, not where I'm from." She laughs and looks out the window. "Did you see his face?"

I did. Smiling, I joke, "I think Amber lost her fuck-buddy."

As if summonsed, Amber appears in the bathroom doorway. Her hair is wrapped in a towel and she's wearing a ratty old robe. She rolls her eyes when she sees us. "Get out of here, bitch," she says to Mel, which was a mistake. No one says that to Mel.

Mel walks over to her and growls in her face, "What'd you call me, you little piece of—"

I tug Amber's arm. She doesn't move. I hiss in her ear, "That was like the worst thing you could have called Mel. All those rumors about her growing up in the hood are true and you just pissed her off. You might want to run before she rips your face off."

Amber comes to life. She frantically mutters things that make no sense and finally says, "I have to go." She races out the door in her robe and doesn't come back.

I hug Mel and say, "I owe you one. Thank you."

She nods. "What are friends for if they can't chase off hoes and guys with little winkies?" We both laugh. Mel turns to leave and says, "Get dressed in peace. I'll check in with you in the morning. We can have pancakes. I'm running a syrup deficit."

I watch her walk away. Confidence lines her shoulders, even though her life has sucked. It's made her stronger and she's better for it. I'm done moping. I'm not letting my past consume me. I don't care what it takes. I'll survive because I want to—on my own terms. Fuck everything else. I deserve a happy life.

# 40

AFTER I'M all decked out for work, I feel strange. It's like part of me wants to turn cold so I can endure this fate. The other part of me whispers in the back of my mind, telling me that things can still be warm and safe. I need to smack her over the head with a frying pan. That little voice in the back of my head is going to ruin me. She never stops hoping, even when there's nothing left to hope for. I gag that fragment of my brain and lock her away with my pride. Tonight is about getting to tomorrow. It's about surviving and that's it. Nothing else matters.

My dress swishes against my bare thighs as I take the stairs two at a time. My Chucks are on my feet in case I have issues with my car. There are always issues with my car. If I really take more clients, like Mel encouraged me to do, I can replace the misfit car with something that actually runs. I'd like that. But maybe not. This car is one of the only connections I have to my father. I worked on it with him, taping it up when it dumped oil all over the driveway. It's always been a bad car, but maybe I'll keep it anyway.

As I round the corner, I run into Amber. She's sitting on the stairs with her face in her hands, all hunched over. I came this way to avoid people. As it is, I got three catcalls walking down the hallway and one was from a girl. I pause. There's nothing I'd like more than to kick Amber and run down the stairs laughing, but I don't.

I sigh dramatically and sit next to her, ignoring the dirty floor and my insanely expensive dress. "Hey, bitch," I say teasingly. "Why are you hiding in the stairwell?"

Amber lifts her face. It's covered in a sheen of

tears and snot. Gross. I hand her a tissue. She takes it and looks at me like I'm insane. "Are you here to gloat?"

"No, I came this way so no one would see me spray-start my car. It's parked at the end of the building in that dark lot. As soon as I put the hood up, guys flock over like I'm too stupid to start my own car."

She snorts, "Yeah, well..." I can tell she has something nasty on her tongue, but Amber swallows it and looks sheepish. "You have more guts than me. I've put my hood up, if you know what I mean, just to get a guy to talk to me."

"Yeah, I realize that. You're a prickly bitch when you want to be, but it's like you're bipolar or something because there's a sassy smart mouth in there too. I'm guessing she lost that battle of the alter egos."

Amber holds onto her knees and dabs her face with the tissue. "Yeah, something like that. It's easier to get guys to like me when I act like that."

"You know they don't really know you, right? I mean, if that's not really you. At this point, I'm not really sure who you are."

"Me neither," Amber says. Turning her head

toward me, she looks at me and finally sees me. "What are you wearing?"

I shrug, suddenly feeling nervous. "Nothing. I have a date and can't wear heels driving my car. It stalls a lot."

"I heard you chased down some dick who stole that car out from under you." There's an expression on her face that I haven't seen before —respect.

"I did. Several times." Wonderful, my legacy is being the crazy chick that chases a car that's well past its expiration date.

"I wish I had guts like that. It's like you don't care what people think of you." There's a far off look in her eye, like she can't fathom being that way.

I don't know how to answer her. My life is a mess. I stand and say, "The room's empty if you want it. I won't be back tonight." I start to walk down the stairs.

Amber calls after me. "Where's your crazy friend?"

"Out," I call back, and then I'm out of sight. I don't understand that girl. Awh, hell, I don't understand anything. I should really stop trying. I spend half my life trying to get a grip on things, but they just slip through my fingers in the end. I'm lucky I know my ass from my elbow. There's no clear-cut answer for anything anymore.

The air is crisp and cold. My breath makes little white clouds the moment I walk outside. I tug my ratty sweater over my head, carefully not to mess up my hair. I think about the way I felt earlier today, the way Sean called me on torturing myself with the weather. Maybe I should stop doing that. I don't know. It's one of the few comforts I have. How fucked up is that? Freezing myself is comforting. Damn, I need a shrink.

I spray the can of ether and slam the hood shut. Jumping in, I start the car. It warbles to life sounding like a spastic birdsong. I rev the engine and back out. The car doesn't stall once on my way to Miss Black's. Tonight might not suck so much after all.

Holy hell, was I wrong.

## 41

I STRIP AND WEIGH IN, again. It seems redundant since I was here last night, but since Sean let me leave for the middle of the day, Miss Black does everything again. I'm wearing the same dress as yesterday. I didn't have anything else.

Miss Black holds it out and shakes her head. "This is a major infraction." She takes the dress and tosses it onto her chair. It sits behind her desk getting wrinkled. I'm standing in front of her in my freshly laundered lingerie from the other night. She's not happy about that either.

"I haven't been paid, yet. I took this job because I'm broke. This is all I have."

"Yes, well. Be glad that we have some wardrobe for photo shoots." She plucks something from her closet. "Put this on." It's a tiny black piece of fabric that looks way too small to be a dress.

I eye it and do what she says. As I'm wiggling into the dress, Black takes a box from the bottom drawer of her desk and unlocks it. She removes cash and the book I saw the first night that I was here with Mel. I barely have the dress on when she says, "Leave it. It's supposed to sit high on the thigh, but this—" she tugs the neckline, straightening it. The dress is form fitting. I feel like a sausage shoved into a balloon. There's no way I look hot, but I don't comment. The black dress clings to me. There's a keyhole opening that reveals my cleavage. The skirt hugs my hips tightly and barely covers my panties.

"There, that's better. Now turn." I do as she says. Miss Black grabs my shoulders and I stop. I feel her gaze on my back. She thrusts her hand forward. "Give them to me. You can't wear that kind of panty with this dress. Panty lines are ungodly."

I freeze. I am not going commando in this tiny skirt. "I don't think—" I start to say, but she cuts me off.

Snapping her fingers, Miss Black huffs, "No one cares that you were prude, Avery. Hand over the panties so we can get on with things." Reluctantly, I shimmy them down and fork them over. I tug at the hem of the dress, but Miss Black slaps my hands away. "Leave it. Oh, and before I forget, here's an advance on your paycheck. Spend it wisely." She hands me several large bills. I reach for the money and stuff it in my purse.

Miss Black continues, "You can pick up your clothes tomorrow when you check in. One more thing before you leave. Here is your next client." She turns the big book toward me and points to a page. "I need you to update your preferences sheet and sign."

I glance at the papers. The man is a little older, but still attractive. He's not Sean. With every fiber of my being, I don't want to do this, but I have no choice. I lift the pen and sign the contract. There. Done. I start to walk away.

Miss Black stops me, "Avery, your preference sheet?" She pushes it toward me and sits down behind her desk. I look back at the paper.

"I don't care. Whatever he wants."

Black looks at me like I don't understand what I've said. "Avery, dear, I think you'll—"

"I don't care," I say more pointedly this time. "Whatever he wants. It's all the same to me."

Black smiles like she won the lottery. "I'm pleased to hear it. You'll fetch a higher price with that attitude."

I smile back at her like I'm excited, but I'm not. I leave the building and duck into the limo waiting at the curb. I slip back into my seat and slouch. I pick at my nails for a moment and then stop so that I won't ruin the polish.

How quickly things change. A few nights ago I was so nervous that I nearly puked. Now, I just want to go and get it over with. Staring out the window, I remind myself that this isn't real. It doesn't matter what Sean says or does—this isn't love.

# 42

I HATE how short my dress is, but I walk with confidence, the way Miss Black told me to, as I step into the elevator. When I emerge, the hotel restaurant is in front of me. I pass the hostess at the podium and wave at her, like I'm here every day. Lately, I've been here too much. She nods and I walk into the restaurant, past poshly decorated tables to find Sean seated in the same location in the back. He has that look on his face, and the same dark intensity lurks behind his eyes as the first night.

Lifting his gaze, Sean runs his eyes over me, taking in every curve. His lips don't move. There's no expression on his face. I don't sit. Instead, I stand there, waiting for him to say something. Sean's cold again. This feels like a business transaction and nothing more. Now I understand why he does it. It's because he has to. There's no way to be both warm and contained at the same time.

Sean lifts his steely gaze. I step forward and press my finger to the monogram on his plate. His eyes lock with mine. My heart tries to race faster when he looks at me, but I forbid it. I can be cold, too. I shut everyone else out. What's one more person? I'm not sure why I let him into my messed up life in the first place.

Sean arches a brow at me, but my meaning is clear. Whatever happened this morning is gone. Things are back to the status quo now. Sean nods and extends his arm, waving me to sit. "Avery," he says my name like we're strangers.

My stomach feels like I ate a window—wood, glass, and all—and churns uncomfortably. The waiter appears from nowhere when I take my seat. He pulls back the chair for me and I sit down. Sean orders wine and the waiter disappears.

"Nice dress," he says, carelessly.

"Nice tie," I say, leaning to the side, like I don't care. Sean looks stunning. He's wearing a black suit with a black shirt. His silk tie is midnight blue which makes his eyes look bluer than I would have thought possible.

Sean smirks. "I wouldn't have thought you'd wear something like that." Sean is mirroring me. I pretend not to notice. I sit up and tilt my head, making my hair fall over my shoulder.

"Yeah, well, it turns out that I do." I lean closer to him and give him a lazy smile. "Before I left, Black stripped me and stole my panties, so half the work's done for you." I wink and sit back.

Sean is still leaning forward. His cool façade cracks a little. "You're not wearing panties under that?" I shake my head slowly and smile at him. It seems to do something to him, but he tries to hide it. Sean's voice sounds a little too breathy when he speaks. "Well then, it's only fair to tell you that..." he leans closer. I lean in to hear him whisper, taking a sip of wine as he speaks. "I'm not wearing any panties either."

I try so hard not to react to him, but I can't help it. I snort laugh and choke on the wine. It's so embarrassing. I keep coughing and I can't stop. Sean smiles at first and then looks concerned. He moves his chair closer to me, leaning in and placing his hand on my back. "Are you okay?"

I punch his arm and he sits back and smiles. Everyone is looking at us. "You're such an ass," I hiss.

Sean scoots back to his place. The grin on his face lights him up. I can't picture him looking more perfect than he does right now. "You started it, Miss Smith. I suggest you only step up to the net if you intend to play hard."

"Tennis euphemisms? Really? Nothing says highbrow like tennis," I lift the glass and make snobby face. I suck at not letting him affect me. Within minutes of arriving, Sean cracked my shell and is pulling me out, but I can't have it.

"Well, the balls are the right size..." he opens his hands like he's explaining something that would be rational.

I laugh. I can't help it. "Not for you, they're not."

"Flattery will get you nowhere, Miss Smith."

"I already have a free pass into your panties

after dinner, Mr. Jones. I expect my flattery to get me everywhere and then some." I sip my wine again with a smug look on my face.

Sean's expression shifts from neutral to that lazy sultry look that's so damn hot. "Where exactly is the and then some. It sounds titillating." He strokes his chin, drawing my eye to his lips as he does it.

"Check my preference sheet. It's recently been updated."

Sean's smirk falters, but he puts it back. The movement is so fast that I'm not sure I saw it. Maybe I just hope that I did. "Is that so?"

I nod and tap my fingernail once against my wine glass. "You can titillate anything you want. No restrictions. No hang ups."

Sean just stares at me. After a moment, he asks, "Why the change in pace?"

I avert my gaze and trace my finger around the curve of the glass. "Why not? I mean, that is if you're willing to. Unless, you're only into fake relationship kind of sex..." Sean stares at my lips like he wants to devour them. He doesn't speak.

"Oh, come on," I say, leaning closer to him. I take his tie between my fingers and feel the silky fabric with my thumb. Sean looks at my hand and slowly returns his gaze to my face. "You've got to have some fetish or kinky desire, something that you need." I say the last word slowly, wrapping my lips around the syllables.

Sean sits perfectly still, like he's under a spell. It breaks when the waiter comes back and puts our food down on the table. Sean lifts his fork. He doesn't talk about my offer. Instead, he points at me with a fork and says, "Eat."

Dinner progresses in silence. I don't like eating with him. It feels too informal, too personal. He knows what food I like. The meal on my plate wasn't listed on the menu. It's a salty sweet lover's paradise with sweet sun-dried cranberries, sprinkles of feta cheese, and pork so savory that it melts in my mouth. There's some kind of sweet glaze over the meat. I could die. It's perfectly delicious. I chew slowly, wishing that Sean's thoughtfulness didn't appeal to me, but it does.

After dinner, Sean stands and takes my hand, pulling me up. With my heels on, I can look directly into his eyes. They captivate me and swallow me whole. The floor of my stomach falls away. I suck at this. I don't know how I'm supposed to do this and not be affected by him.

Sean tells the waiter to send up the desserts in an hour or so. He takes my hand and leads me to the elevators.

Someone tries to come in with us, but Sean says, "Sorry, better catch the next one." He holds up his hand until the doors close a second later. We're alone.

I glance at him like he's lost his mind. Sean grins wickedly and reaches past me. He pulls the stop button and the elevator goes dark. Sean presses into me and my back slams into the wall. Sean's hands run over my sides as he leans in, pinning me in place. My breath catches in my throat. The darkness in the tiny room chokes me. Panic slides up my throat.

Sean whispers in my ear, "I'm sorry, but you seriously think you can tell me that you're wearing nothing beneath this skimpy little dress and not make me hard the instant you say it? Feel me, Avery. That's what you do to me." Sean tilts his hips and presses into my leg. I feel his hard length press against me from under the constraints of his slacks.

I'm breathing harder and faster than usual. I hate elevators. I can't breathe. The first time Sean stopped it, we started moving again two seconds later, but this terrifies me. Beads of sweat form on my face. I suck in a jagged breath, trying not to scream.

Sean has me pressed against the wall, which makes it worse. I can't see him. I can't move. Voice shaking, I plead, "Stop."

Sean drops my hands and before I know it, my palms are against his chest and I'm pushing him away. Sean steps back. I feel a vacuum of cold air fill his place. He must push the button back in, because the lights flicker on and we start moving again. Nervously, I tuck my hair behind my ear. I wish I could shrink into the corner and disappear. My heart is still pounding like I'm going to die. Elevators are like big caskets. When they stop, it feels like there's no air. My heart nearly exploded. It's not sexy. It's terrifying. And then Sean pinned me. I gasp, thinking that I'm going to be sick.

Sean gazes at me with a strange look on his face. Desire still swims in his eyes. His affection for me doesn't diminish, the way I thought it would. After watching me for a second, Sean says, "I'm sorry. I didn't realize you are claustrophobic." His eyes are burning a hole in my face, demanding that I meet his gaze.

When I look up, I can't breathe. Sean is so intense, so attractive. He lures me in and I never had a chance. "I'm not," I lie. No one's realized this about me. I hate it that Sean does. I try to break the gaze, but I can't.

"Then what upset you?" When I don't answer he steps closer to me. "Was it the way I touched you?" I shake my head. I know where he's going with this.

Swallowing hard, I answer. "I just didn't expect it, that's all."

Sean nods and seems to accept that as my answer. It isn't until later that I found out that he didn't accept it at all.

## 43

SEAN UNLOCKS the door to the penthouse. I follow him into the room. My heart still beats too fast, too hard. When Sean throws his keys onto the hallway table, he follows me into the room. Taking my hand, he leads me to the center of the room. Sean closes the space between us and presses his body against mine. He starts to sway slightly, like we're dancing. I wrap my arms around him and hold on loosely. His hands slip over the back of my dress. I feel his fingers cup my butt before finding the hem of the dress insanely close. Sean's hands smooth over the outside of my dress and he looks at me. I know he's aroused. I don't have to feel his pants. I can see it in his eyes.

My heart thumps in my chest when he looks at me like that. My entire body responds to him and prickles. I want to feel his hands slip over my skin.

Sean seems to read my mind. Without breaking eye contact, he slides his hands down my sides, feeling my little black dress. When he reaches the hem, his hands move under the fabric. He pulls me closer and slides his hands around back, feeling my bare ass. He responds instantly. I can feel his dick pressing into my belly. The sensation warms me in a way that makes my insides pulse. Why do I react to him? Can't I just let him fuck me and not care?

The thoughts vanish along with every other logical thing in my brain. Sean dips his head to my neck and finds the place that makes me weak. He presses our bodies together, still swaying his hips gently against mine. One hand is firmly holding my butt and squeezes hard while the other drifts around to the front. He lowers his hand between us and dips his fingers between my legs. The response is instant. I moan and fall into him. I can't stand when he does that to me, but Sean makes me remain where I am.

"I expect you to stand here and do what I say," his voice is deep, commanding. It makes me want to obey him. I shiver, wondering what he's going to ask. "Pull up your skirt."

I inch the fabric up until he tells me to stop. My bottom is revealed in all its naked glory. Sean's eyes darken and fill with a carnal gaze that makes me too hot. "Legs apart." I shift my feet. "More."

I move again and now they are shoulder's width apart. Sean kneels in front of me. He presses his face against the V in my legs, breathing in deeply. He stares at my pussy for a moment, like he's trying to control himself, but he fails. Sean dips his head and licks the seam of my lower lips. I nearly jump. "Stay still, Smith," he scolds me.

To make sure I don't move this time, Sean holds onto my hips. When he lowers his head and licks me, every inch of my body flares to life. I gasp as his tongue strokes my sensitive folds. A spark ignites somewhere in my core and I want more. I need more. I hate how he does this to me, but I let him. Sean detected the parts of me that respond the most. That spot on my neck, I didn't even know it was there. It's nearly all the way around on my back, but Sean found it. One kiss there makes me so weak and so turned on. It's hard to not want sex when he kisses me there.

And now, this sexy man is on his knees at my feet doing the most divine things to me. I can barely stand. One more sweep of his tongue and my knees buckle. Sean stands and takes me over to the bed. That's when things change. He removes his belt and binds my wrists together. He explains what he's doing, what he needs. "You're right. I didn't call Black to play house with someone. I need something. I want this." His breaths are jagged. My heart races faster. I let him tie my hands before I realize what he's saying. Looking in my eyes, he asks, "Tell me no now if you can't do this."

"I don't know what you're doing," I confess, feeling afraid and stupid. My heart slaps against my ribs so fast that I think I'm going to stroke out.

Sean's eyes are so dark. Whatever he held back the last few times he was with me is coming forward. "I want to tie you down and have my way with you. I want you at my mercy. I want you to fight back."

I look into his eyes. I don't understand. "You want to rape me?" That can't be what he means, but after I say it, I see the look on his face. I know it's what he wants. My heart pounds harder, faster. "Sean—"

"Say no or yes. Nothing else. You asked what I wanted. This is what I want." His eyes penetrate me. There's a desperation in them. It tells me that he's barely in control of himself. I nod slowly. Tension lines Sean's neck. His hands tighten into fists. "Say it. I have to hear you say yes. I don't want to hurt you, but I might. Sex is power. I need to feel that right now. Avery," he breathes my name like he can't imagine taking another breath if I say no, "tell me what you want."

Sex is power. He needs to feel like he has some control over his life. I look down at my hands knowing how this is going to make me feel. I hate being pinned down. If he ties me up, I'll scream, but that's what he wants—complete power over another person. He's so fucked up.

And so am I, because I say, "Yes."

I don't have to say the word twice. Sean grabs me and throws me down on the bed. I try to roll away, but can't. Sean stretches my tethered hands above my head, straddling me as he moves across my body. Fear pulses through me. I can't move. I can't breathe. He reaches over the side of the bed and grabs something—a rope—and ties my hands down. I know he can't stop and I don't want to make him, but I'm scared. I don't know why. He's made love to me several times. This is not love. It was never love.

I twist and kick out at him. Sean grabs each foot and ties them to each bedpost so that my legs are splayed. I'm face down with my butt hanging over the side of the bed. Sean moves slowly toward me. I want to tell him to stop. I want him to stop and say he loves me. I want something besides this, but this is what I offered.

Sean's hands tug up the dress, revealing my naked bottom. Without warning, Sean thrusts into me. I cry out, not ready for it. I can't move. I can't do anything. Sean pushes in hard at first, gripping my hips and pushing frantically. After a few minutes, maybe more, he slows down. I'm not wet enough. What he does hurts. I whimper even though I try not to make a sound. Sean stills.

It doesn't feel good. Having him inside me doesn't feel like anything. He pulls out slowly. I want to scream.

This is what it's going to feel like with the other clients. I press my eyes closed, waiting to feel Sean pushing into me again, but I don't. Opening my eyes, I look for him, but can't see him. I hear his jagged breathing somewhere behind me.

A tear escapes from my eye and rolls down my cheek. I feel his eyes on my face. I know he sees it. My stomach clenches tight. I close my eyes willing my tears away. No more fall. No more will come. It doesn't matter what he does to me.

But Sean doesn't touch me again. I hear him sit down hard behind me. I struggle with the ties, hoping to free myself, but I can't. Before I realize what's happening, Sean's there and he unties me. I watch his face as he unties his belt from my wrists. He won't look at me.

I stand and rub my wrists and fix my dress. My heart is pounding. "You didn't have to stop."

"It felt wrong," is his only reply. Sean sits in a chair and hides his face from me. The way he leans forward, placing his elbows on his knees and resting his forehead on his hands makes it impossible to see him.

"Why?" I know I shouldn't ask that question, but I do.

Sean looks up at me with such sorrow in his eyes. He doesn't answer me. Instead he tells me more things that I don't want to hear. "Before, when we were in that elevator, when you made that noise—I knew you were afraid. I sensed it. It turned me on faster than anything else. You know why I don't want to do this right now? Because it's not enough, it's not pushing you all the way into your darkest fears. Tiny space with no light terrifies you. All I can think about is fucking you in there, making you so frightened that you scream while I fill you with cum." Sean's breathing hard, like the idea is too appealing to resist. My heart beats harder, faster. "I was like you, once. I felt things by touching and tasting, but not now. I can do those things, but I crave the other so much more. We're a bad match, Avery. I'll break what's left of you. There's very little holding you together. I don't want to be the guy that turns you into this." He presses his fingers to his chest.

I'm stunned. I don't know what to say. Fear

surges through me. I want to run, but I need to stay. "So, you need to hurt me to get off?"

Sean shakes his head after a moment. "No. I need to feel your heart racing and feel you trembling. It's the fear. I need your fear." Sean doesn't look at me. His confession weighs on his shoulders like he can't stand.

I don't know what to think of him or his needs. I can't fathom his life or this. The only thing I can think to say is the thought that keeps popping up in my mind. "But I'm afraid of you anyway." Sean's eyes cut to mine. I feel the world shift.

The words that I'm never supposed to say come pouring out of my mouth in a flood too fast to stop. "It doesn't matter what you do or what you say, I'm desperately afraid of you, Sean. Everything about you seems to bring me back to life. Your voice, your words, your face...I can't think when you're there and when you're gone, it's worse.

"When I saw you this morning, I was torn apart. I'd found your note, the one in your pocket. I thought you were cheating, that you had a wife and a baby. When you showed me her grave, I almost wished you were cheating. I could have walked away from that, but not from this. And that's what frightens me more than a dark elevator or a tiny closet." I hold my breath and try to stop the flow of words, but they don't stop.

I step toward him, almost afraid to touch him. The moment feels so brittle, like it could snap. "You evoke things in me that I've never felt, that I never thought I'd feel. And that's just it—I feel around you, and it's amazing. I've been numb for so long, wishing that I could seal off the pain that's seeping into my soul. Then you came along and I fell for you. I love you, Sean. I can't help it. And it terrifies me." Wide-eyed with a pounding pulse, I watch him react to my words.

Sean's eyes lock with mine, but he says nothing. He just looks at me. It's the worst thing he could possibly have done. A moment later, he turns and pinches the bridge of his nose. Sean doesn't look at me when he says it. "I'm going to tell Black to send me a different girl. You can go." His words feel like a knife to my gut.

I stare at him with a million thoughts racing through my mind. He doesn't love me. The thought beats me down into a bloody pulp. I can't stand to look at him. Saying nothing, I cross the room and grab my purse. I take the stack of bills that Miss Black gave me. I don't think about it. I just act on my feelings. This whole fucking charade can stop. I don't want his money. I don't want him. I want every trace of his existence scrubbed clean from my life. Anger builds inside of me. I need this money, but I need my sanity more. I fling the stack of bills across the room. The money flutters through the room like a gust of oversized snowflakes. Before Sean looks up, I'm gone.

My eyes sting horribly, but I won't cry. I take the elevator to the lobby. He doesn't come after me, chasing me like this is a movie. No, Sean is calling Black now, telling her that he wants someone else. I leave the hotel grounds, not concerned about my bracelet. Nothing can protect me from this. I obliterated what was left of my heart. I feel it dying inside my chest.

I stand at the curb for a second, too hurt to think. The limo isn't here. I'm freezing in this tiny little dress with no coat. I know that feeling, but now instead of providing comfort, it makes me feel sick. I walk, not going anywhere in particular. I pass people on the sidewalks and wish that I was someone else. I have nothing. No one. I spilled my heart, telling Sean exactly how I felt and he returned me. My cell rings a moment later. It's Black. I don't answer. I walk on, going nowhere, thinking nothing.

The frigid air numbs my skin and I welcome it into my heart. The numbness over takes me, and I hope that I never feel anything ever again.

# THE ARRANGEMENT

## COLLECTION B (VOL 4-6)

Continue reading the *New York Times & USA Today* bestselling series now by clicking the link below. This series has sold over 13 copies worldwide and been translated into five different languages. This series is complete with 7 novels total.

## THE ARRANGEMENT: COLLECTION B (Vol. 4-6)

## COMPLETED SERIES BY
## H.M. WARD

SEXY SUSPENSE & THRILLERS

THE ARRANGEMENT

THE PROPOSITION

SECRETS & LIES

TEEN PARANORMAL

DEMON KISSED

# CAN'T WAIT FOR H.M. WARD'S NEXT BOOK?

Let her know by leaving stars and telling her what you liked about this book in a review!

## ABOUT THE AUTHOR

H.M. Ward continues to reign as the NEW YORK TIMES, WALL STREET JOURNAL, & USA TODAY bestselling author with over 13 million copies sold, placing her among the literary titans.

Ward has been featured in articles in the NEW YORK TIMES, FORBES, and USA TODAY to name a few.

This native New Yorker resides in Texas with her family, where she enjoys working on her next book.

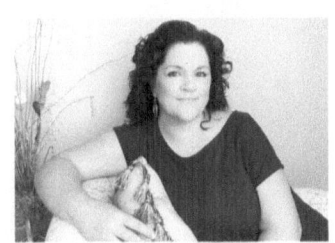

*You can interact with this bestselling author at:*

www.hmward.com